Puppy Lo·

Her Secret Menage·

Text © 2020 Katelyn Beckett

Cover by Enchanted Ink Studio

Her Secret Menagerie

Sadie's Sanctuary #2 Rescuing Us (Releasing for the Holidays)*

Book 4 Simply Purrfection (early 2021)*

*= Upcoming Title

Dedicated to all those striving to find their happy place in life. May you love where you land.

Chapter 1

Sadie

I sighed and tried to crank the car for the third time as the wind gusted against the cardboard-and-tape window. The weather had called for a blizzard last night not hurricane-like winds. Though October was a little early for snow, it wasn't entirely out of the question. My poor car creaked to life and meandered through the front yard, reaching the frosty driveway.

Calls came early in the cooler months. Whether people were worried (rightfully so) about a dog out in the chill or if it were something as simple as a cat sneaking around, I was asked to rectify it. The county was too broke to build an animal shelter, so my home served instead.

That meant I had a collection of pets, all of them a little bit different from the others. The big perk? There was no one else for anyone to complain to when the dogs decided to have a howl-off at 3 am.

I pulled up to the Jenner's house with another, quieter sigh. I didn't want to get out of my warm car. I didn't want to set foot on their property; not after they'd threatened to run me off at the end of a shotgun the last time I'd been over. The law had backed me up and we'd taken care of their chickens against their will. The poor things had been malnourished and too weak to fly.

The Jenners hadn't been able to afford to feed them. I understood poverty all too well. I was always one injured dog or sick snake away from eating ramen three times a day; if I could manage that. It didn't matter. There was no one else to do my job. The animals needed me.

"Sadie Faye what're you doin' out here in this miserable weather?" called a man with corded hands and knobby knees. He made his way over to me, a smile on his face. It hadn't been Mr. Jenner who'd run me off.

It'd been his wife.

I locked the car behind me, just in case, and fell into the accented cadence of my childhood. "Amber said you guys got a pup last night? Some little ratty thing, doesn't look like it's been fed real good?"

"Aw, he's a good boy. Growls at ya, lifts his lips and shows you the cutest puppy teeth you done ever did see. 'Course, he don't look quite right. We're thinkin' he might be some kind of coyote or coydog. The Martins on down the road, they breed them coydogs you know."

The Martins on down the road did no such thing, but it was much easier to agree with him than to deny him the decades-old blood feud with his neighbors. "I'm sure they do, sir."

"You wanna come on in and warm up, getchu some coffee before you head on back down the road?"

I folded my hands behind my back and looked around the property. There was the abandoned chicken coop, the shed that held their old beagle, the ramshackle garage that always seemed to be just this side of still threatening to fall down. "Is your wife in?"

A cloud appeared on that man's face. "She done up and run off to her momma's house for the weekend, all tore up over the fact that I wouldn't let her just shoot this here pup. Didn't seem right to do after the kids had seen him and he was so small."

"It's illegal to shoot wild animals that don't pose a direct threat to you in Clareton County, Mr. Jenner. It's a good thing you stopped her. I'd hate to have to turn her in to the local cops, let them have them have their say on it."

My accent folded up under me as I spoke. It was something I just hadn't quite killed off in all the years I'd tried. Clareton County wasn't the most progressive or the most extravagant place in the state. The local schoolhouse was still a single class, for all I'd graduated at the head of it.

No matter how hard I tried, I still sounded like some ignorant redneck once I got around the locals.

That wasn't to say they *were* ignorant rednecks. They were just country folks trying to squeak out an existence. Sure, it meant that trapping and fishing, growing weed and selling the occasional questionable prescription was sometimes the difference between paying your electric bill and not. But that was just fine so long as you kept it on the down-low or the low-down or whatever it was. Sometimes? Both.

"Well, I wouldn't wanna go messin' around with your laws, Sadie. Come on in. We'll go see the pup in a few minutes. You look plum tuckered out and it's too damn early for you to feel like that."

I sighed. Again. God, it was going to be that kind of day, wasn't it? I gave in with all the good grace I could muster. "I appreciate it, Mr. Jenner. It'd be rude for me to reject you, seein' as how you're so polite."

He held the door open as I walked past him. The house smelled faintly of mildew, but it was in that manner that all old houses do. Doesn't matter how much you care for them or how little you put in; once a house has aged for a while, there's a certain scent to it. And that scent is rot.

It can be pleasant in an old, homey sort of way. My great aunt's house had been like that before it'd burned down. I missed it every day.

"Two sugars and some fresh milk off that little goat farm." He offered out a pink cup that looked as if it'd fallen directly out of a Tupperware catalog.

I took it with a nod of thanks, blew on it, and sipped. The coffee was surprisingly clean and refreshing. I'd expected something... less so.

"Now like I was sayin', Louise wanted to shoot this pup. Said she figured it was diseased or infested, that it'd go and make old Henry sick by keepin' it around. But I just couldn't let her do that," he said, fixing his own coffee as he spoke.

"That was kind of you," I offered around my cup, wishing I could just go see the pup and leave. Louise Jenner wasn't wrong; if the pup had distemper or another easily spread disease, I needed to get on it.

He shook his head. "I had me a raccoon when I was a kid. Tore the shit outta me until we made friends. I figure this pup's just the same. He don't know we don't mean no harm. Probably ain't never had a friend in his whole life."

It was becoming more and more likely they'd caught some coyote and I was going to be stuck rehabbing it. Worse, if it was a fox, I'd have to put it down myself. There was a rabies warning in effect for the species within the county, with one too many showing up on farmers' properties as of late.

Still, I swallowed down my coffee as quickly as it would go. When I was done, I toyed with the handle of my cup. "If we could see the pup, sir. That would be best. I have other calls to get to."

He frowned at me and grunted, pulling himself out of his chair and nearly losing his jeans; which were at least a few sizes too large for him. As I said, I understood poverty and I wasn't going to judge him. But I did make a mental note to gift him a nice belt from the trade day sale in the very near future.

Mr. Jenner led me outside and around the back. I couldn't help but keep one eye behind me, as if Mrs. Jenner was going to show up and shoot me. It was stupid. If she'd run off to her mother's, she really wouldn't be back until she'd cooled down. Our neighborhood was well separated from each other, but the Jenner household fights were legendary.

The live trap was a well-oiled, well cared for device. It made me feel guilty for leaving two of mine in the rain for the past week, attempting to capture a weasel that kept trying to eat my chickens. I was sure my springs were rusting while I stared at the pup within the bars.

Small, pointed ears led into a face that was entirely too intelligent. His tiny, black eyes stared back into mine and I felt as though I was looking into a deep, thoughtful pit of knowledge that identified me as a potential threat. I stayed back from the white and black pup even as I pulled out my cell phone to get a picture. It was amazing what a post on social media could do to help someone locate their lost dog.

...Assuming the pup was lost to begin with. I got the feeling that he was well aware of what he'd done, where he was, and perhaps even how to escape his current confines.

"You want me to take him with me?" I asked, already knowing the answer.

Mr. Jenner chuckled. "Unless you're willing to overturn those laws of yours."

"They aren't my laws, but no. I don't want him put down. If he's sick, we'll do it at the vet," I said, reaching for the cage.

Inside, the pup twisted around in a knot and hunkered. His ears lay flat and he gave me a look that said he had no interest in becoming my pal. I didn't bother him, instead wiggling out of my jacket and draping it over the cage. My teeth chattered. "I'll bring it back for you once we know something about him. All right?"

"Sounds good enough t'me. You just watch yourself and don't let him bite you. He's a rascal."

Without answering, I headed back to the car. The pup got the back seat. I kept a tarp back there just in case I picked up something wild and unassociated with the comforts of modern life. There were a lot of cases like that, especially in the winter, and I liked to be prepared when I could. Thankfully, this was one of those time. I wrapped the seatbelt around the cage, clicked it into place, then headed for the driver's seat.

The drive home was absolutely silent and my dread grew. Few wild animals would remain quiet in that pup's situation. It made sense for him to be sick. Most parents wouldn't just abandon their pup in the wild. I looked in the rearview mirror. "Pretty quiet, aren't you, little fella?"

A kind voice could bring around most animals. Instead, I heard a grunt and a squirm as he flopped around in the trap. That was a bit more promising. He should be trying to stay away from me, but I'd have expected more fight in him.

I hoped that he was just incredibly cold or hungry and not something worse than that.

Upon getting home, I unstrapped him and carried him into my house. "Bosco, Carrie Ann, Matilda, I'm home!"

But there was no response. Only three dogs had gotten the honor of running around loose when I wasn't in the house. The rest went to their crates and were let out upon my return. It was then that I noticed there was no cavalcade of barking, no yowls of glee, no twittering from the parakeets. There was nothing.

I put the trap down and ran to check my gas stove, terror swamping me. I always made sure to remove the knobs so none of the cats could turn it on while I was gone, but had I forgotten in my haste to get out the door? No, the knobs lay on the counter beside the stovetop. And, after that panicked moment, I remembered that my carbon monoxide detector wasn't screaming at me.

Then what was it? I moved through the house, looking for anyone who had come to greet me. Eventually, I found the giant brindle-and-white boxer mix trembling in the mudroom. He had his head pressed into the corner, his back to the door. I went to him.

"Boc-boc," I said, crouching down beside him. "What's the matter? Did someone do something scary while I was gone?"

The dog wouldn't so much as look at me. That, more than anything else, worried me. Bosco loved his nickname, snorfling and rolling all over the ground when I used it. As it was, the dog acted like I'd kicked his puppies. Thoughtlessly, I reached toward him and tried to comfort him.

Bosco snarled at me, drawing his lips back in a show of force I hadn't thought the dog had in him. Internally slapping myself for daring to spread potential disease, I got up and scrubbed up to the elbow with the soap nearby. The sink was a deep, thin plastic box but it was perfect for getting those bad stains out of dog beds and cat tower parts.

Those messes came with the job. When you had animals around, there were going to be gross things to deal with. The average person wrinkled their nose over picking up their pet's poop from a sidewalk. I had a dumpster taken away every two weeks to help keep everything neat and tidy.

As it was, Bosco perked his ears up and looked at me as I cleaned myself up. He came over and hesitantly sniffed my pantleg, then worked his way up the rest of my body. Smiling, I lowered myself back to my crouch and offered my hands out to him. The soap bottle said I smelled like raspberry lemonade, but Bosco must have smelled something else. He buried his big, blocky head against me and slurped my arms until I was thoroughly saturated.

Carrie Ann and Matilda appeared in the doorway as one, not unlike the twins from Psycho. They were both Great Danes, simply massive in size but goofy in stature. The pair were harlequins, the black and white motley types that seemed to be a favorite for commercials. Though, I had to admit, neither of these two would be shown on television any time soon. They were a little too skittish for that.

"Come here, girls," I called, my voice low and sweet.

After a moment's pause, the duo crept over to me. Carrie Ann was the stronger of the two, her mind more set in her ways. Matilda, on the other hand, belly-crawled across the floor and buried her face against me. I ran my hands over her enormous skull, careful of the freshly-healed scars from her past life. Not all dogs got good homes, but the ones who didn't usually ended up with me.

Whatever it was bothering Bosco, Carrie caught a whiff of it from my clothes. Her ears flopped backwards and she moved away from me, whining at the top of her lungs. I tried to follow her, but ended up with Bosco's arm- foreleg wrapped around my own leg. The girls ran away as I got up to pry Bosco from me and, once I got him off, he trotted away, too.

It was so strange to not be welcomed home by boisterous, loud dogs. While Matilda was likely to sneak and creep when she wasn't feeling her best or brightest, I'd never seen Carrie Ann or Bosco react to anything as they were now.

I headed back to fetch the trap, deciding it was best if I got the pup to the quarantine room while I tried to sort out what was going on in my personal life. Maybe there was mold in the ceiling. I'd heard from more than one vet that it could make your pet behave strangely; but it certainly hadn't been there that morning.

No, the only change was the animal in the trap.

"Are you some kind of wolf-dog?" I asked him.

The pup let out a tiny, squeaky howl in return. I kept myself from laughing. The sound often put off wild animals because it was rather aggressive from their perspective. After all, how often do you find yourself reading that someone "barked" out a laugh? We personify it as an aggressive gesture without realizing how we're doing it.

You learned a lot about human communication when you started dealing with wildlife.

I picked up the trap and took him downstairs. When I had inherited the house, the basement had been nothing more than a mold-filled nightmare ready to suck the rest of the building down with it. I'd spent months fixing it up, building sun lamps and bringing the wiring up to code to support them.

As it was, the basement looked as though it were a moderately sunny day outside. Fodder trays stood open and ready to deal with a puppy's particular applications and there were hideaways throughout it. The bleach stomp bucket stood ready for use. I kicked it out the door so I'd be able to disinfect upon leaving for the rest of the house.

I knelt on one of the larger fodder trays, putting the trap down in front of me. A few feet to my left was an old cat tree piece that was shaped like a tube. It was the perfect place for the pup to flee if he was feeling overwhelmed, but still allowed me to grab him if he got aggressive with himself.

"There's no reason to keep you in there until your vet visit," I said. "We're going to take it nice and slow, all right?"

The pup didn't answer. I slid the cloth from the top of the trap and opened the door. The pup sat staring at me for a few moments and I had to admire just how cute he was when he cocked his head a certain way.

All of a sudden, he raced out of the trap, scampered up my arm, and sank his teeth into my shoulder.

I screamed.

Chapter 2
Hudson

I paced the marble floor, my thousand-dollar shoes tap-smacking across the surface. As the world wound up to its first morning challenge, I stood still in the darkness of last night.

Somewhere in my mind, the moon still shone overhead. It was the last night of our Lady's cycle, the climax of all Her monthly returns. Three glorious nights each month, when we had to use the bodies She gave us in all Her wisdom. When we, as men, were truly free to become what we were inside, the sky presented Her in all Her full glory.

And I had lost my son during Her peak.

What kind of an alpha lost his son during the fucking full moon celebrations with his pack?

I'd known it was a bad idea, but I hadn't been able to find a sitter for the evening. The change would have placed me too close to typical humans, the temptation too great. Humans were scavengers that had risen beyond their natural order with tools and minds ever so impressive. Yet, their flesh yielded with little difficulty.

That was forbidden. An accident with a human had cost my pack most of its members long before I was born. No matter what else, it was the most dangerous incident known to wolf kind.

"Still nothing?"

I whirled on the alpha who had walked in on me. So much like me, he was tall with olive skin and dark eyes. His hair was longer than my own stiff, severe cut. His brushed his shoulders. Had I been in my true form, I would have wrinkled my muzzle at him. As it was, I settled for a sneer. "It's not like I can tell the cops."

"And you're stuck here because of meetings all day, so you can't go back out into the country and see what you can find?"

A pair of donuts and a cup of coffee blacker than night had appeared upon my desk. It was what family did for one another. I walked back to my chair, spun it around, and sat. Then I looked up at my assistant. "I can't go back out into the country because we killed those sheep last night and if I smell their blood again, I'll-"

He shook his head. "Eat your donuts and drink your coffee. I'll call their local animal control, see if he's turned up. It's not like he's going to shift back."

"But what if he does, Gabe?"

If my son revealed what we were, showed the world that we'd only gone underground instead of falling away to the distant memories of humankind, it would be a hellstorm. The government would test the boy, at best, and find out he was related to me. They'd hunt down my pack, perhaps use us to find the other packs spread around the United States. We'd be in for it, and it would be all my fault.

Just because I was a worthless father who couldn't keep an eye on his boy.

And that was to say nothing of what our own community would do to us for violating the Supernatural Secrecy Pact.

To his credit, Gabe rolled his eyes at me. "If he does, we'll pay the PR guys to explain it away. We're already all over those rags with Elvis sightings, anyway."

"Not us, personally. That was the Little River pack down in Louisiana and-"

He cut me off. "I know not us personally, but it could be in no time. All it takes is a game cam in the right neck of the woods, you know that. We bought all that property out there, but a few gates and no trespassing signs don't stop determined poachers."

My nails dug into the glossy wood of my desk, my jaw clenching. The idea of poachers on my land, my pack's soil, hunting our animals and befouling our earth? Fluffy white fur sprouted across the back of my left hand, creeping up my wrist and into the sleeve of a suit that-

Gabe slapped the spot beside the coffee and shoved it at me. I caught a whiff of his frustration, like burnt toast and mud, and wrinkled my too-human nose at him. Did he want a fight? In the middle of the office? Because if so, I was certainly in the mood to oblige him.

"Drink," he ordered. "Drink or I pour it down your throat when I call Leo and Xav in here. You're all worried about the kid and here you are, practically snarling at me in broad daylight."

I growled at him, but I took the coffee and swallowed half in one gulp. It scorched its way down my throat and into my guts, promising a revolt. The second sip was much more befitting a man of my dignity, a human who worked a comfortable couple-billion-a-year job and owned a few too many cars. I sat the mug down and let out a slow, healing sigh.

"Better?"

"Get fucked."

"All the time," Gabe promised. "Once I find a girl that can handle this."

He emphasized the last word with a thrust of his hips and the motion of his hands down his body. I snorted at him and picked up one of the donuts. "You got me strawberry-filled."

" 'Course I did."

"I hate strawberries," I said, trying to hide my amusement.

Gabe flashed me a smile and glanced at my now-bare left hand. Satisfied that I wasn't going to ruin the secretive world of werewolves to the general public, he swished his tail out of my office and left me to work.

...Alone.

As much as the work paid, as much as I found satisfaction in it, I had to admit that my office was more of a cage than anything else. But Gabe had promised to look into the matter and I had no doubt that he would do his best to hunt him down.

When we'd started making dog food, it'd been easy. Hell, we hadn't even needed to have dogs in the kitchen to test it. One of us transformed, shoved a few bites in our mouths, and told the rest if it was a decent meal or not. More often than not, we'd spent only a few days on each formula.

We were a smash hit. Dogs ate our food like it was prime rib. There had been reviews that dogs had torn into cabinets and refrigerators to get to our kibble and our canned mush. I wasn't the biggest fan of the kibble; it left you feeling a little dry no matter how much water you drank afterward. But some pet owners just couldn't keep up with the demands of wet food, and those nutrients were important regardless of how the pet set got them.

I spent the next few hours screwing around on the computer. I checked a variety of social media sites, hoping that someone would post my son. Maybe they'd given him a bath, shoved some food in his mouth, and snuggled him up in a pile of cozy blankets. I was supposed to be browsing over the monthly fiscal reports, but my boy was out in the wilderness and who knew if he was safe or not?

He stood a better chance than most kids who got lost outdoors. His fur was plenty warm for the colder evenings so I wasn't particularly worried about freezing or frostbite. Better, he knew his way around the property we owned out in the unincorporated portion of Clareton County. But he was still vulnerable. Predators didn't usually toy with a werewolf, even a pup, but owls and hawks took a chance now and then.

The idea of Tommy in pain or injured set me on edge again. I took another stiff hit from the coffee and killed the donuts in a single go. The sticky strawberry mess looked enough like blood to soothe the animal inside of me.

What I really needed was a steak and, after the shareholders meeting that afternoon, I'd have one. Even if I had to rip it off a big, buck deer with my own teeth.

Just before lunch, I forced myself to look through the reports. The numbers swam together on the screen but I made myself work through them. Profits were up. Expenses were down. Everyone would be pleased and the meet shouldn't take terribly long, then. Hopefully, no one would want to push a point of trying to lower expenses even further. We'd made good deals with the farmers who supplied our various protein sources and kept them afloat in a world where meat came from the grocery store.

Too often, humans had forgotten that their meat had to moo and wander a field at some point. We visited every farm we signed. We looked for those who were on the verge of losing their property due to taxes or disaster; floods were hell on a beef farm and we'd had plenty of them over the past few years.

More so, we tried to support the farms we felt were doing the right thing. Slaughter day was never a happy sight, but we preferred the animals who had only one bad day. When you run on four paws, you come to have a sense of companionship with the rest of the fur and fang club. Ethics mattered.

We'd turned those ethics into a multi-billion dollar company in only six years. No matter if people thought that their beef came pre-packaged from day one or not, they cared that we looked into the backgrounds of the farmers. They cared that their pets were getting only the finest meals we could produce.

They cared that our pet accessories were made from products that we would use ourselves. Hell, the labels on the first bags had been pictures of us as wolves. I'd been slapped on the beef and amaranth bag. My eyes were still part of the logo.

Of course, no one knew that other than the pack. ...And perhaps the other rare werewolf who kept pets. There is something about stark, golden eyes that, when authentic, catches another werewolf and holds them. We know our own kind even when it's a static picture on a bag of dog food.

I'd seen it happen once when I'd been touring a new facility. We'd hired without checking too deeply into those who would be working there. One worker, a young woman, had stopped when she saw the bag. Her hackles had gone up, her eyes had widened. Female alphas were rare, but not entirely unheard of. And she'd seen the challenge in the photo of my gaze.

Lillian Webster, said a ghostly voice. That's my name. Is there a problem?

There had been so many problems after that introduction. I ran the tips of my fingers over the keyboard one last time, then locked the program and stood up. I stretched and tried not to think of the alpha bitch that danced across my thoughts. Lunch was ready, and that meant meeting with the rest of the pack.

Our hallway was cut off from the rest of the building. Sixteen floors, all of them filled with our workers, we kept our stature small to keep spending limited. There was no reason for a skyscraper when we didn't need it, though finance constantly seemed like they were bouncing at the idea of expanding.

"Hudson! You joined us! Here I thought you'd gotten lost."

Leo was the sort of family you chose, not the type you were born with. I shook my head at him and he mocked me, shaking his shaggy blond hair back at me. He was five years my senior, in his middling 30s, and built like a fortress. But those wild, forest green eyes brought the ladies to him every time we walked into a... ...hell, take your pick. Parties, bars, even promotional venues had him with three, four, even five girls clinging to him at any given time.

It was ridiculous.

"Where's Xav?" I asked, walking to the buffet that catering had been so kind as to provide us with.

Mostly? I concentrated on the beef. The bloodiest steaks, the thickest cuts. They knew that we were passionate about our protein and they delivered every single day. I really needed to give our catering crew a raise. They did such an incredible job. I made a mental note to do so when I got back to the office.

Gabe came up to refill his plate as Leo ignored me. "He's stuck talking to one of our vendors. You know how hands-on he is."

"Little too much. That's what he's got his assistants for. Is it that big of an issue?" I asked

He rolled his shoulders in a not-quite shrug. "He says it is. But he promised he'd show up. No dice on Tommy, by the way. But nobody's complaining about chewed up chickens or anything like that, either."

I nodded, because it was all I could do. Gabe kissed me on the cheek and I followed him back to the table, tearing into my steak as I sat there. It would do me no good to starve myself. Tommy wouldn't appear just because I was hungry, and if anything? It might distract me when I did have a chance to go pound some dirt and look for him that evening.

"If we had a bigger pack, we could have people out there right now," Leo said.

I swallowed the hunk of meat in my mouth and gave him a look. "We had a bigger pack at one point. What happened?"

"They got dead."

I snorted and sliced through another thick cut of meat. Leo spoke up again. "Because of your dad."

"I know what happened. We all do. There's no reason to talk about it here," I said, my tone telling him the conversation was finished.

He didn't take the hint. "Look, I'm not saying it was entirely his fault. But you have to admit-"

"Drop it," I growled, facing him fully.

Leo toyed with his fork and knife, letting them flop back and forth between his fingers. His gaze narrowed and I readied myself for an attack. The fur didn't pop out quite yet, but it was a very near thing. Gabe rolled his eyes and continued with his ridiculously overloaded cheesesteak sandwich. Nothing would stop him from having a satisfactory lunch.

The tension broke when I fell to the ground, convulsing once, twice. Pain, terrible pain, tore its way through my psyche and found an exit through my feet. I moaned, rolling on the ground and tearing at the low pile office carpet. Whatever had passed between Leo and I wasn't important, he was there to grab my head and keep me from knocking into the lunch table until Gabe had it moved out of the way.

Only once before had I felt agony like that. I tried to force air into my lungs. Just breathing had helped last time but this? No, this was the sort of thing nightmares were made of. It was like every nerve in my body had suddenly decided to have a fucking parade, zapping and sparking in ways that I didn't fully understand.

"Easy," Leo said above me. "Come back to us. Talk to me. There's nothing for you to worry about, just me."

I gasped through the agony. "There's plenty for me to worry about. Fucking christ that hurts."

"What's up?" Gabe asked, as though we'd all just met in a goddamned mall food court. There were times when he was a bit too relaxed for my nature.

"Maybe something happened to Mom?" I said, confused. "The only time I've ever felt like that was when Dad bit her, turned her back when I was a kid."

Leo withdrew and sat back on his feet, his brows raised. "The last time you felt like that was because someone forcibly entered your Lineage and you got a link established with an omega. Your mom's an omega, right?"

"Yeah," I said, because that was all I could do. Confirmation.

He traded glances with Gabe and my stomach sank. Unless my father had decided to crawl out of his grave and add a few more ladies to the family, that only left one possibility. My omega mother certainly wasn't going to turn people; it was beyond an omega's powers to do that. Only alphas could give the gift, the bite, that would eventually turn a human from one of those soft, ape-like bodies into the sleek, lithe hunter that worshipped the moonlit sky.

I'd mated with an omega and she had given birth to an alpha. If I dared to say it, that was probably why the kid was such a handful. Alphas had a mind of their own from a very young age, often wandering off when they were only a few months old. We did our best, as parents, to keep them with us but what Tommy had done was absolutely normal in our society. It was why it was so important to teach them young, and to teach them early, to hunt and nest in the wilderness.

And, most importantly, to avoid humans.

Because despite all their soft and gentle natures, humans were terrifying. They had tried to end our race throughout history, hunting us to the brink of extinction because of the actions of a wolf who couldn't control their bloodlust or one who wanted revenge. We only turned those who were pre-approved by the rest of the supernatural community, because doing otherwise was forbidden. It was suicide. And it was wrong, stealing a simpler life from the human and forcing them to learn to be something they weren't.

Of all the different beliefs and belief systems among the packs, flights, prides, and such of the world, it was the one truth we all held. It was a law beyond all others. We were never meant to turn those with no understanding of the supernatural world.

And if my hypothesis held true, my son had just broken that law.

Chapter 3
Sadie

I pried the pup off of my shoulder and held him at arm's length. He wagged his tail at me, bloody tongue lolling out of his mouth as if he were proud that he'd nailed me. It wasn't the first time I'd been bitten by an animal and it certainly wouldn't be the last. Once, an opossum had managed to get me and the county hospital had demanded I get rabies shots.

Everything you've read about them? Absolutely true.

God, I hoped this little rascal had a rabies license.

He squirmed out of my grip and I had to dodge another playful snap of his jaws, this aimed at my legs. I got up as quick as I could and backed my way out of the room. Thankfully, he didn't seem to understand stairs. He whined at the bottom of them, scratching at the last step with his tiny, needle-sharp claws.

One of the first things they teach you during puppy training classes is to ignore a whining, screaming puppy when they're in their comfort zone. Not knowing how long I would have him under my guardianship, I thought it best to start crate training in a positive way. I tossed a handful of treats into one of the grassy squares and shut the door behind me. He'd have to use his nose to find the snacks and, as young as he looked, it might take him a little while to figure it out.

As for me, I went to the nearby bathroom and pulled my shirt away to examine the bite. He'd certainly broken the skin, the injury far deeper than I'd ever had a puppy hurt me before. There'd been a fox who had come close, though, and I hadn't told anyone about him. Sometimes local vets were a little too enthusiastic, wanting to test the brain for rabies rather than wait ten days for signs of the disease. I wasn't about to let that happen to a fox who had simply been defending himself, so I'd put him in the rabbit hutch out back for ten days, provided food and water, and let him go when I was satisfied he hadn't killed me.

That had been years ago, so I was pretty certain he hadn't been rabid. I still had the scar on my hand, I noted, as I flinched at the oozing wound on my shoulder. It didn't look bad enough to require stitches, so that was a plus for the pup. I cleaned it, winced my way through smearing antibiotic ointment on it, and plopped a gauze pad over it. Then, using some roll gauze, I wrapped the wound from armpit to clavicle. Stretching and flexing my arm didn't move the hack job I'd done, but it did make me have a certain Revolutionary War motif that I couldn't shake.

"Well, I'm not the flutist," I told Bosco, who came to sit beside me as I worked. "I failed band in high school. Who fails band, Boc-boc?"

He wiggled his stump of a tail at me, but his face held a note of worry that would have been missed by those who usually referred to him as "just a dog". I leaned down and kissed the top of his head. That stump wiggled harder, enough that I had to encourage him. "You keep that up and your whole butt is gonna wag right off."

Bosco took a moment to process what I'd said, but when his three whole brain cells rubbed together, he woofed at me and ran out of the room. His hind legs tucked under his belly and he scampered as fast as he could across the kitchen floor. The poor guy missed the carpet, caught it with one forepaw, and went skidding off into Carrie Ann and Nicodemus, a grouchy old centipede of a corgi that had gotten out of his crate, apparently.

It was possible, I admitted as I stared at the pile of dog, that Carrie had let him out. She knew how crates worked and the pair of them were absolutely the best friends that existed in the whole house. As it was, I shook my head as Nicodemus snarled at Bosco and the boxer mix got up, shook himself off, and hurried off to go find someone else to pounce on.

I worked my way from the kitchen into the living room. There were nine crates in all, most of them older dogs who had been abandoned or had been requested for pick up. The owners couldn't afford their medication or special food for them; or maybe they just couldn't deal with the messes. Lady, an elderly cocker spaniel who'd been named after the old Disney character, had peed on her pee pad. When I'd gotten her, she'd been a nightmare of crate messes. All she'd needed was a pee pad to help her out if she couldn't hold it.

But that had been too hard for her 90-year-old owner to cope with, and I understood that. I stroked Lady's head and let her out into the yard to play with the other older dogs. Nicodemus went zooming past, his tail up in the air. I scooped the little guy up and knocked him into my sore shoulder.

Hissing, I carried him back to Carrie Ann. "You aren't goin' out there to antagonize Lady, Nic. You stay right there and be a good boy."

The dog wagged his tail at me and flopped down on Carrie Ann's bed. I took a moment to clean up Lady's mess and replace her pee pad with a fresh one. Few people believed it just wasn't all that hard to take care of my menagerie, but when you stayed on top of things? It was no big deal.

Speaking of which, I reached for the hard floor mop and did a quick once-over of the kitchen. After that, it was the work of minutes to vacuum the carpeted living room. Everyone's water bowls were topped off, as was the communal water fountain. It was time for brunch.

And there was absolutely nothing in my fridge that looked good.

From greens to fish, I frowned at all of it. I shoved past the mashed potatoes, reached around the brussels sprouts who had seen better days, and briefly considered the cooked, tube-shaped chicken dog food I kept on hand for Lady's bad days. The stuff looked and smelled like salami and I was tempted but even I hadn't sunk that far. I hoped.

I pulled open the freezer and my eyes locked on the first thing I saw. There was a massive old steak with a thick bone running down the center of it. The t-bone had been a gift from a neighbor when they'd butchered one of their cattle last year. Though there was a little potential freezer burn on it, I drooled at the thought of a steak. Just the red flesh melting between my teeth was almost too much, but the idea of gnawing on that bone, breaking it between my molars?

God, it was better than sex.

I tried to shove that word out of my mind. Between neighbors asking if I was interested in their sons (I wasn't), and strong men who turned up to donate things like old dog kennels flirting with me, I had plenty if I ever wanted it. The simple fact of the matter was that none of them shared my passion. They looked at animals like they were lower than the dirt beneath our feet. None of them would have tolerated Lady's problems or the cockatoo that shrieked curse words. That cockatoo had found a wonderful home, but I still had memories of him screaming at me at the top of his lungs.

Almost no one wanted to deal with that. And that's why he'd come to me.

Besides, men weren't as loyal as the animals I helped. I'd had my heart broken so many times, it just wasn't worth the effort.

"Easy, Sadie," I told myself. The steak slid out of the freezer with just a little tug. Delicious.

I popped on one of the dials and clicked the gas on. It sparked and the flame quivered in the morning light. It didn't matter that the steak was frozen. I liked my meat blue, when it was safe to eat it that way. The butter knob skittered across the cast iron pan and I put the steak down without bothering to season it.

The meat popped and crackled like wet wood. Okay, maybe it did matter if the damn thing was unfrozen or not, but it just meant a stiffer crust. Right?

"Sure," I said. "Yeah. That's how that works. I'm positive."

I had no idea how it worked.

"Yes, you do." I stirred the butter and the accumulating drippings, basting the steak again and again. Then I turned up the heat. A hotter pan meant good things, didn't it?

Why was it so hard to concentrate? Why was I questioning myself so much? I made great steaks, but the science felt just out of my reach. It was like I was losing my mind.

I sighed. "Time to do it the old-fashioned way."

The meat thermometer was hidden in the endless reaches of my kitchen utensil drawer. I pulled it out and stuck it in the middle of the steak. Then? I waited.

And waited.

I absently rubbed my shoulder, the pain not so deep as it was before. The slight discomfort distracted me from staring at my steak and pulled my mind around to the pup downstairs. I'd moved the electrical, the plumbing; anything high enough that Carrie Ann and Matilda couldn't reach it. Yet, they'd never managed to land a bite on my shoulder, either. ...And maybe the pup was hungry.

After all, a few treats weren't much on an empty, young stomach and it wasn't as if I could finish the entire steak myself. I checked the thermometer and, satisfied that any pathogens were probably long dead, pulled it out and gave the steak a quick flip. I let the other side sear for a moment or two, then flopped the whole thing onto a plate, grabbed a fork and knife, and headed down to see the pup.

He wiggled at me from the bottom step, still too frightened to try the stairs. I didn't blame him; I wasn't much of a fan of them either. The dogs of the household would get the drippings from the pan and the pup would get a proper meal of puppy kibble that evening; but it seemed sensible to try to make friends with him.

I sat down on the floor after heading down the stairs. The pup jumped for the plate, but I gently pushed him back. "Ah, ah. We don't do that."

Amazingly, he sat down beside me at the mere utterance of "ah ah". Someone had bothered to train him a bit, at least. I used my lap as a table and cut the ribeye section of the steak into tiny, bite-sized pieces. The rest I reserved for myself.

Not wanting to get bit again, I tossed the first bite to him. He gobbled it down and ran for the plate again. Another simple voice correction and he hurried to sit once more, his head tilting as his ears folded against his head. Weirder, it was if I felt how badly he wanted it, as if I wanted to wiggle back at him and tell him it would be just fine.

Piece after piece, we got the entire steak down together. His tummy bulged in just the right way and I made a quick mental note to let him out for potty time in the next hour or two. The pup leaned against me, rubbing his face clean on my shirt. Knowing it was stupid, knowing it was a bad idea, I reached out and petted him along the chest, careful to avoid his neck. I didn't want him to think I was threatening him.

The pup yawned and nestled against my hand, choosing to rub his face on it instead. I watched, smiling down at him. A moment later, he shoved his back into my leg and flopped over, already asleep. No matter how much my instincts wanted to stay, to keep watch over the pup while he snored, I couldn't. I had other matters to attend to.

Throughout the day, I snuck him out into the quarantine yard to let him relieve himself. He was an absolute gentleman. So, what had that bite been?

It worried me.

"Unpredictable behavior," I told Carrie Ann, "is one of those terrible ways we know that dogs are sick. Did you know that?"

I pulled the pup's pictures off my phone and posted them to the local lost and found social media groups. Several people cooed, a few sneered that I was harboring a wild animal, and one in particular sent me a message with a picture of his cock. Lovely. As my social media window dinged with dumbasses, I pulled up a search engine and started to flick through photographs of wild animals, trying to nail down who my little friend was.

"Well, he's not a fox. Doesn't look much like a coyote, the color's all wrong and so's the muzzle," I muttered.

Bosco snorted at me. "Bawruff."

"I'm just trying to narrow down my options."

"Snrff."

I rolled my eyes, returning to my screen. "Everyone's a critic."

Still, the closest thing the pup looked like was a freaking wolf. That was impossible, unless someone had bought one from one of those exotic pet auctions? Wolves were absolutely illegal in our state. ...But the exotics auction was the next state over, where everything was wild and free; or at least, it was for sale for people with the money to buy whatever they wanted.

I didn't think that applied to my local area. Not everyone was dead broke, but sometimes weirdos dumped strange animals where we lived. The cursing cockatoo had gotten an African Grey friend in that way, when someone had simply thrown out a big, biting bird to try to live on his own. I'd managed to save him and get him into a rehabilitation facility for parrots a few states over, but the Grey had made life interesting for a couple of weeks.

My social media window dinged again, the message sound this time. I paused before clicking on it. If it was the dick guy again, I was going to send a report to the administrator of the group. Who knew if that guy sent those kinds of pictures to kids or not, and there were plenty of them involved in the group trying to help out the animals.

I believe you have my dog said the message, but I was captured by the profile picture.

Hudson Fontaine was a gorgeous man, a mixture of English and French while looking like neither of the two. He had wild, dark hair atop his head and brown eyes that were just a shade away from amber. His jaw was strong, covered in stubble, and his nose... didn't fit either. It looked like it'd been in more than one fight. But men that wore jackets like the one he wore in his picture? They didn't do their own fighting. They lived in towers, a million miles in the sky and away from people like me.

The intensity in his face said one thing; he was a man who was used to getting what he wanted. And some feral part of me curled my knees together and demanded I lower my head to his wishes.

I scanned through his profile, most of which was private. However, there was one neat tidbit. The guy was a founder at Fontaine Feeds. His company kept every single one of my animals happy and healthy, though I paid through the nose to make sure it happened.

"Maybe he'll give me a couple of coupons or something," I murmured as I typed. *Do you have any proof of ownership, sir?*

The answer was stiff and direct. *I have his paperwork. I can bring it with me, along with my private veterinarian.*

That's fine. So long as it identifies him as yours, I'm happy to return him to you. Where would you like to meet?

There was a pause and several instances of typing, another pause, and then more typing. I tilted my head at the screen. What was so difficult about a question like that?

I would prefer to meet where he is. He is a difficult dog to work with and if he has been destructive, I will reimburse you for your suffering. I recommend handling him with gloves and doing so at a distance.

The rescue is located at 24091 Highway 24 South in Paulinesville. You may have to use 24091 24th Street SE to make it work on your map app I typed, shaking my head. It was always a pain to get people all the way out to the house, and I needed dog food in the next day or two, anyway. I could have just made a trip of it, gone into town, and delivered the pup there.

Of course, that posed a problem if Hudson was lying to me. But why would he? He had to be richer than anyone out here could dream of being. Men like that didn't steal random dogs off of social media.

And your preferred time, Miss Adelaine?

The pup would probably make a mess overnight. I drummed my fingers on the desk and hoped no one called me at 3 am again. *Any time after 8 in the morning is fine. Just send me a message when you're on your way, if you don't mind.*

8 am it is. We will see you then.

I updated the status of the post, noting that the owner was likely found, and rubbed at the wound on my shoulder again. If the pup was so fierce, I wondered what his owner would be like.

Chapter 4
Hudson

I whipped on my most intimidating tie, the morning sun peeking above the horizon just beyond the city. No matter what, I would get through the ordeal that reared its ugly head this bright, chilly day. My son would be home. Whoever had been bitten would be treated with the medication Gabe had procured.

When all of this was said and done, it was entirely possible that my son would owe his life to his adopted uncle.

A brisk walk past Tommy's empty crib felt wrong. I paused, turned around, and went back to make sure everything was comfortable for him. His favorite bear, heavily chewed, sat comfortably against one corner. The top came down to lock, keeping him where he belonged when I was asleep. He was coming to an age where he'd need a larger bed, one appropriate for a toddler, but I hadn't been able to locate one I could lock or build a kennel around.

After all, I would think anyone would understand if they knew the boy. Look at the scrap he'd already gotten himself into; gotten all of us into. There were procedures, rituals, long respected and absolutely necessary to change a member of human society into one of ours. And he'd happily skipped off sideways, doing whatever he wanted.

I smoothed his blanket, glanced over my shoulder, then pulled it up to my nose and inhaled my son's scent. Puppies have an innocence, a newness to them that is so clear, so crisp. Like the first day of spring, they're filled with hope and dreams. My inner animal whined, confused as to why I hadn't already gotten my pup back. I held it in, refusing to cry in this absolute solitude.

Tommy would be home soon. That would have to do.

The blanket was replaced, tucked into the corners and left. I went down to the kitchen and snarled when a fork tapped one of my stoneware plates, spinning to face the intruder who dared-

"You always busy huffing baby blankets, Huds?" Gabe asked, poking his omelet. "There's one for you, too."

He sat comfortably at the breakfast dining table. The abandoned high chair caught my eye for a moment but I made my gaze settle on Gabe, instead. "You could've said you were breaking and entering this morning."

"Could've, should've, didn't," he said, pointing at the still-hot skillet with his fork. "Go eat so we can get a move on. You're not sensible when you're hungry."

"Okay, *mom*," I grouched, grabbing the pan, a plate, and flopping the ham and cheese omelet onto said plate. I stalked back to the table and flopped down beside him.

No coffee this morning, I noted, but orange juice instead. It was probably for the better. I didn't need caffeine to set my nerves on edge. I jangled enough already.

Gabe took his empty plate off to the sink and rinsed it off. "So, it's some kind of rescue organization? That's lucky. They probably won't sue for whoever he bit."

"You felt it, too?"

"Not as strong as you did, I'm sure," Gabe shrugged as he sat back down. "But strong enough. Lillian might've, too. She could drag us in front of a Meet."

"She won't."

"You don't know that."

I stuffed the last bite of omelet in my mouth and glared at him. "She won't. She's not going to risk her nephew. Besides, our contemporaries don't care what a single pack does to a single human."

"Always look on the bright side of life," Gabe answered me, singing the words.

My glare deepened. "If she does call a Meet of the local supernatural community, we'll deal with it then. You got the pills to reverse that human's transformation, anyway. We can present a rectified situation and that will make anyone happy."

"Except the dragons."

I rolled my eyes and took my plate off to join his. "The dragons are never happy about anything."

"They've been through a lot."

"Not as much as we have," I said, grabbing my coat and my keys.

Gabe snatched the keys and jingled them in my face. "Much more brooding, scary billionaire if you show up with a well-dressed, handsome driver-and-possible-lover attached to you."

I cringed. "We're cousins."

"She doesn't have to know that. Come on, ladies love a little guy-guy action, and you said she was hot."

"I said she was an attractive young woman in her late 20s, perhaps early 30s, and that she had steel in her eyes. I said that I was concerned she would sue us if her employee became ill, Gabriel," I growled.

We walked out the door together, him hooking an arm in mine. I scowled at him, but I didn't shove him away. If I were being honest with myself, which I wasn't, I had basically said that she was hot. She was. That didn't mean it meant anything. We'd have my son from her, make certain that whoever had been bitten wasn't going to sue, and maybe make a nice donation to the rescue. If you gave people something up front, they were less likely to sue you in any case; even if it was less than they would win in court.

The drive was peaceful, scenic, and everything you could want from a late autumn trek into the wilderness. We got caught up in the morning commute for a few minutes before Gabe whipped us out of the city on some side trek that had far fewer people trying to swim upstream toward us. The clientele would complain about our early morning absence. They could wait. I'd gone to the shareholders meeting, been blessed over and over again by our investors, and then gone home early yesterday.

Fontaine Feeds did not need me to sit in my office every waking moment of every workday. We'd been beyond that for a while now. Yet, taking Gabe with me was a lot to ask. Leo could handle everything that Xavion couldn't. Not accounting for my pack, the rest of the staff were good humans with good heads on their shoulders. The building would still be standing when I got back to it.

"Nothing's fucking labeled this far out," Gabe snarled, poking his cell phone as it told him to turn around, again.

I leaned my head back against the headrest and tried to compose myself. "Try the alternate address."

"I've tried every damned address."

"Have you tried the rescue's name?"

Gabe stopped on the dirt road and looked over at me with the flattest expression. He picked up the phone, entered *Paulineville Animal*

Sanctuary one letter at a time, and clicked a button. The phone happily informed us that we were at our destination. I frowned at it and got out of the car, cast a furtive glance in either direction, and lifted my nose to the wind.

Springtime, touched with cinnamon sugar and berries. There were dogs, so many dogs. They were our kin at some level and I recognized them immediately. I walked a short distance back and found an old dirt path half-hidden by trees, just about the size of a vehicle. There were recent tire tracks in the soft earth.

"Ah, hidden driveway," I muttered. "No postal service this far out, I suppose." I lifted my head and waved my arm in the air. "It's back here."

My cousin stuck his head out the window and stared at me, as if I were asking him for the world. I waited and, eventually, that head withdrew and he backed up the few hundred feet and a little past me. I slid into the passenger seat once again and we made our purposeful advance onto the property of PAS.

It was more than I'd expected. Clean, happy dogs ran in a yard full of obstacles and play equipment. An old Great Dane danced around a Cocker Spaniel carrying a stick that was half the size of the smaller dog's body. I stepped out of the car and the play stopped.

Cats yowled, birds shrieked, the dogs threw themselves at the fence and roared as one. I took another step backward, blinking. These were not the typical idiots I ran into along the sidewalks of the city. These beasts knew what I was, the missing link between wolf and man, and they weren't having it.

Well, they would need to learn to.

I walked, silent, up to the fence. The elderly Dane snapped her jaws at me and I smelled it upon her, the reek of imminent decay. She was not long for this world and though she knew it, she was ready to take me with her. I had to hand it to her that it was a brave thought, a powerful one. She wanted nothing more than to protect her caregiver and the rest of the dogs.

My hand reached out, ignoring those big teeth, and came to rest on her head. "Easy, girl. I know. I don't blame you."

The dog fell silent, staring at me with a confused notion on her face. She didn't understand, didn't gather why she wanted to tear me apart; only that she did. In her youth, she had been much more frightening. No one had dared cross her. Yet now she was losing her place among the dogs and the fact that I had taken control so easily wouldn't help that-

"Are you here for the puppy, sir?"

Gabe let out a low whistle. I didn't notice him join me, but I damned sure noticed her.

The woman stood there with her head cocked to one side, her dark hair up and out of the way. She wore a simple sweater tucked carefully over a pair of corduroy pants the same dark blue as her eyes. In her hands, she held a coffee mug that steamed in the morning cold.

And when she smiled, my whole world stopped.

My son frolicked around her ankles, like a cat who'd found a new best friend. I looked around at the dogs, who had fallen mysteriously silent at her appearance, and hopped the fence; magnificent suit and all. Tommy came running to me, his tongue falling out of his mouth. I picked him up and held him, not caring that his paws were muddy or that the dry cleaner would never get the dirt off.

He smelled like springtime just after a rainstorm, the first promise of flowers and fawns in the meadows; exactly as he should. I rubbed my lower jaw over his head, protective and reassuring. But there was another scent that caught my attention, too. It was that cinnamon sugar and berries, touched with cream so close up, the release of heat from a summer storm brewing overhead. There were fallen leaves and the warm, familiar scent that I only knew as pack; a sensation that rooted itself so deep in me that I could not begin to explain it. It was belonging. It was family. It was home.

And it was *her*.

The sweet scent of omega rolled across me, my son covered in it. Had she been holding him? Rocking him so he would quiet down after a fit? God, had he shapeshifted in front of her? He couldn't have. The conversation wouldn't be anywhere near as calm if he had. I lowered my head and gave my son a soft huff just to be certain I had it right, but there was no denying it.

"Well, no doubt he's yours," she said, leaning heavily against the stair's railing.

I tried to regain my composure. She was the one he'd bitten. God. What was I going to do? "I appreciate what you've done for my dog. Did he give you any trouble?"

"I thought he broke the skin when he bit my shoulder yesterday, but it's just bruised. No harm, no foul."

"If I could see, ma'am?" Gabe asked, moving forward.

"Are you his vet?"

Gabe didn't bother to ask me. "Yes ma'am, perhaps I can help you figure out what really happened."

As Gabe reached for her, I stepped between them and stared him down. "She said she was bitten. Let's leave it at that."

He frowned at me. I turned my attention back to her. "Ma'am. Miss Adelaine, isn't it?"

"It is."

Her tone had gone frosty, her skin paling. I glanced back at Gabe, who moved forward to offer her a hand. She shook her head at both of us and walked backward. The dogs began to growl once more and I was deftly aware of their presence behind the two of us.

"I don't know who you are," Sadie said. Her hand came to rest on her forehead, as if she were checking her temperature.

My cheeks flushed as her scent washed over me again. I clutched Tommy to try to keep a handle on myself. I wanted to pursue her, stalk her like the prey animal she was. I wanted to sink my teeth into her neck and show the world that she was mine, only mine, that she'd taken my kno-

The presence of other werewolves was exciting her inner beast as much as it was mine. I doubted that Gabriel was having any easier time with it. He was as much alpha as I was, the two of us sharing the need to lead when it came to it. We listened to Leo and Xavion when it was required, too. Alpha packs had been unheard of at one point, but we were little different than roving bands of unmatched stallions or lions when it came to leadership and, when it came to love.

Tommy's teeth sank into my arm and I grimaced. The pup practically hung from the limb, his lips curled in a snarl. It wasn't as if he were jealous; he was much too young to have that sort of affection for the omega in front of us. I corrected myself; for the soon-to-be not-omega in front of us, a human named Sadie Faye Adelaine.

Even the syllables of her name rang in my ears, offering themselves to me with wide arms and a teasing smile. I tried to shut the wolf up but he wasn't having any of it. Fur raced along my spine and down my shoulders. I pried my son from my arm and lowered my head to hide any wolfish eyes from scaring the woman.

"You don't have to know us. We aren't here to hurt you," Gabe said. "Just to get the pup and leave. Thank you for your assistance. We'll be in touch to discuss your compensation."

Sadie followed his face for the first few words, then I saw her gaze begin to drift. I put Tommy down and prepared for it. I'd been there when my father changed my mother. I knew what was coming, had seen it before. Sadie tried to respond. Her mouth worked but nothing came out of it. The mug flew toward the ground but Gabe scooped it out of thin air.

And I caught her when she fell.

She struggled with me for a moment, her expression untrusting. Then her head rolled back on her shoulders and I peeled off my glove to check her forehead myself. Despite the cool, she was burning up.

Gabe picked Tommy up. "How bad is she?"

"102, 103. Somewhere in there. She's close. She can't go to a human hospital like this. They'll send her to some closed-off ward and run tests. And it still won't stop her from transforming when the moon comes out in a few weeks." I said it all very quickly, but the seconds were moving at a glacier's speed as I held her in my arms.

It had been so long since I held an omega; any omega. I dared not lower my head and breathe her scent, run my hands over her to discover her. I held myself back and let out a slow, quiet sigh even as the rest of my instincts screamed for me to do something, anything, to claim this wonderful creature as my own.

Gabe clucked his tongue against his teeth. "Let me strap this guy in and I'll come back to help you out with her."

"What?"

He shrugged and walked back through the dogs, all of which were eyeing us with that same level of distrust that their owner had displayed.

"We're taking her back to the house, aren't we? Like you said, human doctors are no good. You can't leave her here."

I ran the possibilities through my mind. Her, Sadie, in our home and laying on my bed. I would still have to administer the medication that would force her humanity to shine through, but that didn't have to picture into it for a moment. Instead, I dreamed of a new wolf, a beautiful and tricksy omega that forced me into hot pursuit. She wove through the trees, decorating herself with the scent of the forest as I chased her, knowing that the end would only offer us the potential to be closer than ever.

My cousin was back too soon. He cleared his throat and I, as careful as I could, moved around to grip her shoulders. Between the two of us, we carried her back to the car. I slid off my tie and balled it up along with my jacket, pinning it between her shoulder and her cheek. It would do for a pillow until we could get her home.

Tommy whined, his ears back at me. I reached out and ran my palm over him from the tips of his ears to the bottom of his tail. He curled up, a wolf pup still, in the footwell of the passenger side. He'd already outwitted Gabe's attempt to buckle him in.

"Your place?" Gabe asked as I climbed in.

I watched in the rearview mirror as Tommy snuck out from the footwell to hop up on Sadie's lap. One of her hands absently petted him. I took a deep breath and let it out.

"Yeah. My place."

Chapter 5
Sadie

I awoke to a large man, who I didn't recognize, sitting beside my bed. His hair was jet black, his skin darker still, and his eyes matched the rest. He was built like he could rip a train in half with his bare hands and he leered down at my sleeping body like he wanted to do the same to me.

Needless to say, I screamed.

Despite the rough look the man inspired, his voice was as soft as satin. "Easy there, sweetheart. Easy. You don't know me yet, but Hudson said to tell you the critters are being taken care of. You're safe, they're safe. It's gonna be all right."

The room I was in was nothing like I'd been in before. Riches bedecked every surface, though they were subtle. It was in the well-made nature of the dresser set, or the fact that the bed I lay in was a four-poster style with actual curtains. Though they'd been drawn aside so the man could keep an eye on me (I assumed), the fabric had the sort of texture that you only saw at the expensive hotels; like the Hilton.

"Who are you?" I asked, drawing the blanket up around my neck. At least I'd have padding if he tried to pull me apart.

He leaned back in his chair and the mere movement adopted a friendlier demeanor. "Xavion Fontaine. Hudson's brother."

"Why am I at Hudson Fontaine's house, Xavion?"

He shook his head. "Damn. He wines you and dines you and he's still that forgettable?"

"Pardon?" I asked, dropping my vowels into the low country drawl I'd been born with.

Hudson Fontaine sounded familiar, but I couldn't quite place it. How long had I been out? What had happened to me while I had been out? Why was this giant of a man watching me until I came around? Had I made a complete ass of myself somewhere, somehow? Questions filled my head until I wanted to scream.

Then a familiar puppy came padding in through the door. He raced toward me, leapt on the bed in a single bound, and rolled himself all over the blanket I lay hidden beneath. I picked him up and tucked him under the covers with me, just in case Xavion wasn't a fan of dogs.

"Yeah, he likes you all right. You're the first one, you know that? Kid's not even all that fond of me and I've known him since he was born," Xavion said, rubbing the puppy's head with his knuckles.

I watched as the puppy grumbled and scooted away from him, unable to keep the smile from my face. He was such an opinionated dog, so strange and different. I reached for him only to have him latch onto my hand and bite as hard as he could.

Blood welled in the corners of his mouth, then he yanked away and slid off the bed. I bit my lip as I curled around my injured hand, trying not to cuss up a storm. It was just impolite when you were in someone else's house.

However, in doing so I was in the perfect position to watch as my skin knitted itself back together. It was over in seconds, completely healed and painless.

What the hell had that rich guy given me?

"I want out," I said, throwing my legs off the side of the bed. "I won't tell anyone. I won't go to the news, but I'm leaving this house right now."

"Little one," Xavion rumbled. "You aren't going anywhere."

He picked me up as if I weighed nothing more than the puppy did, then he put me back into the bed and stroked my cheek. "It isn't safe for you out there."

Oh, God. I'd been kidnapped. There were weirdos in Hollywood, but that was across the country. Did we really have people who liked to, I don't know, murder hapless animal rescue women? Was that a thing? Everybody had their own special stuff that made them twitch just right but that wasn't it, was it?

"If you're going to kill me, you better do it before I start screaming again," I threatened.

A smile split his face, broad and sweet. "No one here wants to hurt a hair on your head. Except maybe the kid, but he's got the right idea of it. Gonna take his dad a little while to come around."

"You mean the puppy. Is he a puppy? A wolf cub? Because people really shouldn't go ownin' wolf cubs, especially if they live in a place like this," I said, waving my freshly uninjured hand around at the finery.

The door opened and the man from before, not-Hudson, walked in carrying a tray. "Well. He's a wolf cub. But you wouldn't believe what he really is, even if I told you."

He placed the tray in front of me and I sat up enough to look down at it. "Who are you?"

"Gabriel Fontaine. You can call me Gabe," he answered. "We're going to do a little experiment."

That sounded a little too much like 'would you like to play a game' to me. My friends had been way too into horror movies and I'd caught the bug around my senior year of high school. It tainted a lot of things.

Gabe pulled the cover off the tray and I was face down in it before I knew what was happening. I tasted meat in the back of my throat, blood on my teeth. My hands were covered in it, my hair falling from its straps to the red-tinted plate below. Xavion laughed at me even as I sat myself up and tried my best to wipe up with my sweater sleeves.

"I'd like to see you do any better after being unconscious for who knows how long," I said.

It was Gabe that answered me. "You've been out three days. Your animals are being cared for by the best money can buy. But I'm afraid that you'll be staying with us for a little longer, after that response."

"Why?" I asked, using my tongue to ferret out a piece of meat stuck between two teeth.

"Because you're a werewolf."

I looked between Xavion and Gabe, waiting for the punchline to drop. When it didn't, I laughed until I thought I'd be sick. So what if I'd just devoured a steak in a few seconds? I was hungry, not some mythical beast that shredded Little Red Riding Hood. This time, I slid off the bed and I meant it.

"It's been fun," I said. "But you did whatever you did, starved me for several days, and planted me in your bed." Gabe opened his mouth but I held up my hands. "I already said I won't sue. All I want is a morning-after pill, if any of you did anything."

Gabe glared at me. "That's entirely inappropriate. We might be wolves, but we aren't monsters."

"You guys do whatever you want. That's none of my business. You've got great dog food, by the way," I shrugged, having meant to say it during our initial meeting. "Even Bosco loves it, and he's the pickiest dog in the universe."

"Is that the Dane?" Gabe asked, moving in front of me to keep me in the room.

I glanced back at Xavion to find him still sitting. They weren't trying to force me back into the bed, at least. "He's a boxer mix, white and brindle. Terrified of storms. Carrie Ann's the Dane that kept telling you two off."

"You've got a very loyal pack already, Sadie."

Was it a threat? If I left, were they going to poison my dogs? They owned the dog food company, for crying out loud. It wouldn't be hard for them to deliver a little notice to me by making my animals sick. It wouldn't have been the first time some creepy fuck thought he could do that and make me pay attention. "You touch those animals and it'll be the last thing you do."

"No wonder the kid likes her. She's half a wolf already," Xavion said.

Gabe just sighed. "Miss Adelaine, I won't stop you if you want to leave. But if you do insist on going, I have to require you to take a few tablets before you go. They'll strip of your powers and leave you a mortal once again."

"Oh, so you're immortals and werewolves, now?" I asked.

He shrugged. "Semi-immortals. We can be killed, but it takes a hell of a lot to do it."

"Fine," I snapped, tired of the game. I held out a hand. "Give me the drugs and I'm getting out of here. I don't care if I have to hitchhike home."

Gabe felt around in a pocket for a moment before he produced a little green packet. He dumped the contents into my outstretched palm.

Three grey pills, each with a tiny sliver moon on them. God, at least they had a theme down, right? I tossed them in my mouth and swallowed. Then I showed him both of my empty hands and motioned toward the door. "Took them. Now can I go?"

I'd no sooner said the words than the pain hit me. Falling to the floor, I doubled over and clutched my stomach. Xavion and Gabriel were there in a heartbeat, coming to my side and trying to help me back into the bed. I snarled, swatting Xavion across the chest with a handful of nails, useless and too dull to slash the man as he deserved. Instead, I tried to crawl away from them.

Neither seemed to be supportive of my goals. I was picked up in long, strong arms and carried back toward that bed. With each of Xavion's steps, bone crunched and joints popped. Everything screamed for the torture to be over, for whatever it was to take hold and leave all the rest to fall apart, landing as it had to. I thrashed against his hold, against his chest, and he simply held me.

"That shit is supposed to heal her, not hurt her," he rumbled.

There was a rattle of pills, so loud that I thought my head might explode, and Gabe cursed. "They gave me the wrong meds. I'll kill Yves."

"Yves? You trusted fuckin' *Yves*?"

Gabe snorted. "What was I supposed to do? Disappoint Hudson? Yves was the only guy in town with the stuff to turn her back into a person. It's all regulated now. I can't just walk up to CVS and say hey, you have any anti-werewolf pills?"

Xavion didn't respond, but I felt the growl deep in his chest. He put me on the bed again, the last place I wanted to be, and held me still. I fought, for a moment. His scent hit me in a wave that never quite crested, always ebbing and flowing as I tried to decide if he was the warm, smoky flavor of a midnight campfire or a crisp snowflake melting on your tongue.

When I made up my mind that he was both, another surge of pain spread through me and I clawed those beautiful blankets to ribbons.

In the background, I heard Gabe talking on a phone. The words were meaningless, but he sounded livid. Men as powerful as they were didn't get mad all that often, I thought. They always seemed to have their hand on their lives. They had everything handed to them on a silver platter, exactly how they wanted to see it and when they wanted it.

They weren't used to getting the short end of the stick or getting screwed around; not like I was. I cried out, a weird howl-yelp noise, as my hands shrank before my eyes. Petite paws replaced them, furry white to the elbows and then sleek, wood bark brown. My sweater lay on the floor, lost in the madness I was witnessing. Terror swamped me and I fell to the bed, overwhelmed and not entirely aware of what was happening to my body.

A period of confusion passed. The world seemed a little dimmer, the red faded and weak in the curtains and the blanket. I stared at Xavion, my chest heaving as he stroked my cheek. It was a comforting gesture, but not as kind as other, unknown sensations would have been. I didn't know what I wanted, but I knew that it wasn't just to be petted.

Under the campfire-and-snow scent, there was another in the air. I closed my eyes and breathed deeply, trying to find the source. This one was honey and marshmallows, toasty and rich. Gabe walked over and the scent intensified until I was bathed in it, licking my lips.

Yet there were no lips as I recognized them. My tongue met a muzzle, flapping against the side of a furry lip that I couldn't see. There was dark fur along the snout that lay beyond my eyes, but the rest of me was too tired to examine what I had become. It was something to do with those pills. Whoever these men were, they had formulated some manner in which to become animals.

That technology would sell for billions of dollars to the right people. According to every conspiracy theorist I'd ever had the pleasure of speaking with, every military in the world was trying to create the perfect weapon. A shapeshifting animal that could pretend to be human when it needed to? That sounded like it might make the mark.

"You in any pain, sweetheart?" Xavion asked.

I tried to respond, but all that came out was a mixture of whines and yawns, each sounding more like a dog than the one before it. I finally shut my chops and looked up at him, willing him to know that, while nothing really hurt, I was completely exhausted again. And it was very likely that I was going to hurt before too much longer.

Honestly, if not for the exhaustion? I probably would have run out of the room and taken shelter somewhere. My instincts were already poking me to find a den, drag some soft nesting materials in there, and to hide from the rest of the world. And, unlike my human body, these instincts were strong. A few of them were so strong that I was surprised I wasn't dragging myself off regardless of the discomfort.

Gabe shoved his phone in his pocket and came over to sit with Xavion. "I'm sorry. They mixed up their medication, Sadie. This should have taken care of your transformations permanently, never allowing you to become one of us. Instead, they forced your transformation. And I don't know if there's a way to go back after you're a wolf the first time."

I whined. I'd never be human again? Again, I willed so hard for him to understand me.

"To a normal human life," Gabe corrected himself. "You'll still be a person when you need to be. We'll instruct you in that. But it isn't... typical. You'll be under the moon's eye. That means cycling with the rest of us. There will be changes."

He paused, cleared his throat, and then added, "There will be urges."

I didn't understand. It was though there were some small connection between us, as if it were just out of my reach to use to help him comprehend what I was trying to get across. As I worked to reach for it, the door smashed open and adrenaline flooded my veins. I was up and off like a shot, diving between the men and out the door as fast as my legs would carry me. There was an intruder, a danger, and I had to get away from it.

I ran for the room that smelled like springtime, like the first flower in May and the fresh buds sitting in the new, bright sun. The part of my mind that was still desperately holding on to my humanity noted that it was a child's room with a gorgeous mural painted on one wall. I saw wolves howling up at the moon, four of them in a semi-circle around a fallen deer. The animal wasn't profusely wounded or anything like that, but it certainly looked dead enough for me to lick my lips at it.

There was a crib in a nook of the wall. That was the source of the springtime promises and I crept toward it, my tail tucked between legs that had spent so long in the same pair of pants.

A lid kept the crib closed, which wasn't entirely unheard of for some kids. Those were the ones who went out and accidentally lit their house on fire playing with the stove when their parents were asleep. I lifted my long snout to sniff the inside of the crib and blinked at what I saw.

The wolf pup lay curled up within the crib, one paw wrapped over his eyes so he could sleep throughout the day. I stared at him, confused. Hadn't Hudson called the pup a dog? Was a crib necessary for a dog?

It hit me all at once. The bite, the weird treatment, the medication; it was all part of the same puzzle. It was why Xavion kept referring to the puppy that I'd saved as 'the kid' rather than 'the dog'. It was why Hudson had driven so far to come and get his dog back from the house out in the woods.

I took several steps back from Hudson's son and did my best to breath slow and steady. There was not a mythical world full of supernatural creatures creeping along the outside edge of our own.

But if that were true, why was I running around a billionaire's mansion right now on paws?

I hunkered down on my belly and slid beneath the crib. There, it was dark and it smelled of puppies. My instincts took over and I fell asleep, warm and surrounded by the scent of peace and happiness.

Chapter 6
Hudson

The commotion upstairs was loud enough to put me off my swiss and bacon sandwich. I left the plate, knowing that my son would probably sneak down to steal it, and headed up to see just what the hell was going on in my home.

Gabe ran into me on my way up the stairs. He was incredibly bedraggled for a man of his usual coolheadedness. "They gave me the wrong fucking pills and now she's stuck under your kid's crib, freaking out and chewing on her tail."

"They made her a wolf?" I asked, trying to compute what he'd just said.

He glared at me as if I were an idiot. "No, they made her a cactus. Yes, Huds, she's a goddamned wolf. And I don't know how to get her back. Yves isn't returning my calls and she screamed when Xav tried to reach under and grab her."

"And she's under Tommy's crib?" I blinked. Gabe gave me a jerky nod and I hurried up the rest of the stairs, taking them three at a time.

I walked into a scene that would have been comical, had the girl known that she was going to be a wolf. Instead, Tommy was wide awake and gleefully bouncing around in his crib. Xavion was on his hands and knees, using that same voice he used when we found some woe begotten dog on the side of the road. And in the shadows, just beyond Xavion's reach, was a pair of incredibly blue lupine eyes that were wide and terrified.

Shaking my head, I got down on my hands and knees and prayed my suit would forgive me for it. "Move, Xav."

The alpha, a long-time friend and pack brother, turned on me with a stiffness I didn't care for. Occasionally, alphas got into dick-measuring contests with each other. It happened; it was just part of who we were. But this wasn't the time nor the place for it. I showed him my too-human teeth and stiffened right back at him.

We'd had our differences in the past; all of us had. Even Gabe and I had gotten into a scrap or two over the years when we disagreed strongly on something. Those wounds healed in a few minutes and we'd end up laughing and trying to drink one another under the table. It was how alpha-only packs survived, how we communicated. But I didn't want the omega under my son's crib to get the wrong impression, either.

Xav backed down after a moment to rethink himself. I gave a pleased snort and crept over to stick my head under the crib. Above it, Tommy whined. Beneath it, Sadie trembled.

"You're going to be just fine," I told her. "If you'll come out from under there, we'll talk you back through to your human body. We'll fix it, together."

I didn't know if she would believe me or not. I put every bit of CEO-based iron into my voice, every syllable ringing with alpha authority, but it was possible that her instincts were screaming too loudly to hear it.

Or not. One socked paw slipped out from beneath the crib, then another. Her gorgeous sable-colored head came out, her ears flat against her skull. She stared at me, then began to slide back into the dark, secret place. I had to control myself. I wanted to scruff her, drag her out and growl into her face. I wanted to help her nest in this special cavern she'd found, secure it for pups and-

God, pups? Get a hold on yourself, Hudson.

"You're all right," I said, soothingly. Xavion peeked around my shoulder. Sadie paused, then huffed and shoved herself out.

I reached down and stroked her back, my hands as gentle as they could be. I sat back on my feet and watched as she shivered. "Try to think of yourself. What makes you, you?"

Her head tilted up at me as if I were speaking Latin. I tried again. "If you had to describe yourself in a dating profile, what would you say? Think those things, inside, and imagine your human body."

She whimpered as the first changes took her, fingers lengthening from paw pads. Her legs stretched to become arms, uncomfortable and unwieldy at first, but I didn't stop. "That's right. That's exactly what you need to do. Keep envisioning it. Keep it in your mind. You're almost-"

All at once, she whipped into human form and threw her head back, gasping. She was naked, streaked with sweat and shed fur, and the most beautiful creature I'd ever seen. For all I wanted to admire that wonderful body for a little longer, I reached for the blanket Xav held and wrapped her in it, picking her up and heading toward the bedroom.

"Gonna sue you all until I own the feed store," she whispered, head lolling.

I smiled down at her. "After this, maybe we'll just gift you an entire store. Do you run that rescue all by yourself?"

"Grandpa used to help me, before he passed."

Ah, inheritance. I'd been lucky in that way, inheriting enough from my grandparents to start the company. Yet, it hadn't been a sure bet. And a structure that took so much to run and lived on donations? Her little pet sanctuary was probably constantly on the verge of bankruptcy. Most of them were. We got so many emails and letters, begging for donations to help the animals.

"We sponsor a few agencies, you know," I told her. "We could sponsor yours, too. Make sure you never have a need for anything again, whether it be a set of kennels or just a supply of food."

She didn't respond, she only looked up at me as if she were looking for some reassurance that she wasn't crazy. It didn't feel right to just drop her in bed and go back to my sandwich. I fell into bed with her, drawing her close against me and leaning my shoulders against the headboard, my shoes still on my feet.

"You're experiencing what every turned werewolf does," I said, running my fingers through her hair. It was messy from the transformation, but still soft as silk.

Her expression broke, tears forming in the corners of her eyes. "You guys made me a monster."

"I'm afraid my son made you a werewolf, not us," I sighed. "He's just a puppy. He should have known better."

"What was a child doing out in the cold by himself?"

There was a hint of heat under her words. A protective omega, fierce around the pups. My heart sang but I told it to shut up. We weren't going to get entangled with her. Keeping a professional distance was for the best. "He's an alpha- you know, alpha, omega, that sort of thing from dealing with your dogs, yes?"

"Dogs don't work like that. It's archaic theory from someone who found out that wolves didn't work like that, exactly, either."

I rolled my eyes. "Werewolves work like that."

"Werewolves are bullshit."

That surprised a laugh out of me. "You were just chewing on your own tail in a dark hidey-hole and you say that."

"Well, they are," she said, her voice uncertain. "Maybe I'm just having some kind of fever dream. Or maybe I went crazy. I don't know. People can't be wolves. Werewolves aren't *real*."

I decided to try something on her. I rolled her over onto her back, pinning her down. My weight forced her into the mattress and I stared down into those lovely eyes. She looked away in an instant, baring her throat to me; all that creamy expanse just begging for my teeth to-

Holding my breath, I rolled us back to the side. "Still think it's not real? Do you normally flash your throat at anyone who's posturing at you?"

She was absolutely silent, a frown creasing her brow. I went back to stroking her hair, trying to quiet her. Yet the roll had seemed to do just as much as talking had. The poor thing. It was hard enough being an alpha, but I'd have never wished being an omega on someone with little information about our world. The things she was feeling, the instincts telling her that I was safe and to go snuggle down in the scent of my pup's room? I had no doubt it was overwhelming, confusing, and incredibly unsatisfactory.

Most omega women went into heat on their first mandatory transformation, the first night of the full moon after their bite. Those born as omegas would go into heat upon sexual maturity, usually around the age of twenty or so. But Sadie was in for a rough time if we didn't get some ground rules put in place, and we only had a few weeks in which to do it.

"Listen to me. You are a werewolf. We remain hidden because of what you see in movies and television shows. The wolf always gets the sour end of it. What my son did is illegal in our community. It's why Gabe tried to give you pills that would kill your inner wolf. You'd be as human as anyone else, but it seems there's been a mix up somewhere. You were given medication to help you transform. And we can't have that happening."

I said it all in my softest voice, trying to lull some sense of comfort into her. While omegas were drawn to alphas, it wasn't just the brutal force of protection. It was the ease we gave them. It was the ease that happened to us when we had something worth taking care of. An alpha's sense of self was intricately intertwined with how happy his omega was.

I reminded myself time and again that she wasn't *my* omega, just *an* omega. My wolf didn't care. There was an omega, period, end of story, and she was lost, confused, and upset.

"Maybe if I have a little time to think about it," she said. "It's just so much to take in. First, I'm taking care of a puppy and next thing I know, I'm being recruited to have paws at night."

"Not all nights," I corrected automatically. "Usually just the three peak full moon nights. Less, if there're storms in the area. It's the moonlight itself, Her guiding light, that gives us our true forms." I paused, then added, "And those pills."

She blinked up at me and yawned, covering her mouth. Color rose in her cheeks. She warmed against me, even through the blanket, and I barely restrained a shiver. Sadie had no idea what she was doing to me, that her every movement aroused curiosity and interest in the beast inside me. I tried to think of nothing by abysmally dreadful paperwork to shut him down.

It didn't work.

"Why have those pills anyway? It seems like it's a bad idea," she said, nestling into the center of my chest.

Her eyes slid shut and she stilled. Most people squirm and shuffle around before they decide to go to sleep. Wolves don't. They curl up, tuck their nose behind their tail, and they go to sleep. It was one of the nice things about being in wolf form. You never really needed to find a comfortable spot when your bed was among the willows and the reeds.

"They're for those who want to have a little extracurricular fun when the moon isn't showing her face. Maybe they want to go on a hunt or a walk with a pack mate in the dark. It's far safer to have your fur and fangs on than it isn't."

She mmm'd at me and I peered down at her, moving her bangs out of her face to check that she was asleep. A stray lupine whisker still stuck out at an odd angle from her upper lip, but it was a good overall transformation for a first-timer. I approved. I enjoyed the quiet, her weight comforting and familiar. We stayed like that until the world just had to make a rude intrusion.

My damned phone buzzed in my pocket. Sadie sighed and turned her head toward it, her lip wrinkling to show a single tooth at the sound. I strangled a laugh off in my chest and arched slowly so I could reach the noisy thing.

'That Bitch' splayed across the screen. A headache twinged to life in my forehead, working its way toward the hind of my skull. She was the last person I wanted to talk to while I held some innocent woman. Would my past never die? I answered, my voice low and displeased, "Hello, Lillian."

"Don't take that fucking tone with me, Fontaine. What the hell did you do with my nephew?"

Her voice was like being pepper sprayed across the head of my cock. "Thomas is fine. He took a walk out in the woods, someone found him, and he's home safe and sound. If that's all?"

"That isn't all. What did you do? Who did he bite?" Her voice fell and I heard her take several steps away from wherever she'd been. "I swear to God, Hudson, if you endangered Becca's boy, I'll have your pelt for a carpet."

"Bite?" I asked. "Maybe your senses are getting unreliable in your older years. It happens, Lil. Every bitch I've known has that same problem in their 40s. Sense of smell starts to go, the internal connection with your Lineage is all messed up-"

She snarled across the phone and I shut up, like any rational mutt would. "I know what I felt. I want to examine him, make sure you haven't harmed him in some way. And if I smell a human anywhere on him, I'm calling a Meet."

"You'd call a Meet of all our local supernatural folk just to prove a point?" It wasn't much of a question. Lillian would do it just to try to rip me apart. She had every sensible reason to be angry at me, but I didn't have any way to fix it.

Her voice was poisonous. "I'd call a Meet to see my nephew taken care of. To make certain that you aren't letting him in harm's way. To get custody if I have to and do away with whatever tail you're wagging these days. You're not stable enough to raise a pup. It's like a frat house over there."

"Better than him growing up in a convent."

She sniffed. "The church is misguided, but they care about the treatment given to young boys."

"You're the only nun I know that uses the word 'fuck', you know," I said, needling her.

Lillian didn't need to be poked. "You'll meet me, with Tommy, at the Safeway on Tableton Road in two hours, or the Meet will be called and I'll have him examined by the dragons."

She didn't give me a chance to protest or to try to explain that I had other things to do. She hung up as I opened my mouth and I was met with the wonderous silence I usually preferred after dealing with her. The problem was that Tommy would smell like human for the next few months. Any wolf that attacked a human, though I hesitated to call a puppy nipping an attack, would bear that human's scent for a good time to come.

It was one of the things that made wolves who committed bites so likely to be found. One good whiff from another supernatural being and they knew that you were guilty. Worse, the dragons were the lawyers of our universe. They would judge my son with little recourse other than an eye for the laws laid down between the various species hiding from humanity, and they would be likely to order his execution.

Lillian would protest, citing that it had happened under my responsibility. She would state that I had allowed or encouraged my son to commit the bite and, due to his young age, promote the possibility of it falling on my head rather than her nephew's. She would steal my son and kill me all in one blow, and she would smile as she did it. Hell, if she played her cards right, she might take out the whole pack.

It was all I could do to keep from smashing the phone into the nightstand. I tried to slide out from beneath Sadie, but she didn't want to budge. As I said, when a wolf sleeps it rarely moves around. It makes us slightly less than a sandbag, but not by much. She sighed when I picked her up and plopped her down upon a bastion of soft, squishy pillows that molded to her body.

"Where you going?"

I barely had my shoes on the floor before she was awake. She squinted up at me, that frown present on her face again. I ran the back of my fingers over her cheek. "Work. If you need anything, Gabe and Xav will be here. And if you're very good, I'll bring you something special. How is that?"

"The only thing I want is for you to stay here."

In truth, I think the words took her by surprise as much as they did me. The animal inside me perked his ears up and a flutter of something hopeful worked its way through my chest. I didn't bother to shut it down that time. It felt good, and it'd been so long since I'd had it.

Without thinking about it, I bent over her and kissed her forehead. Instincts kicking in, she lifted her head at the last moment to expose her throat. Our lips brushed, her tasting like almonds and ice cream, my favorite flavor from decades ago. I paused, but she froze. We stayed like that for a few seconds before I drew away and cleared my throat.

"Like I said. Stay here, I'll bring you something back."

And with that, I absolutely did not flee that room before she said anything in response. I merely left.

Chapter 7
Sadie

When Hudson left, it felt like the stars all went out in the sky. I was left in an endless, mysterious void that didn't quite work for me no matter what I did. Everything was different, alive, but constantly changing.

Gabe brought me a ham and swiss sandwich half an hour later. I stared up at him as he approached, my instincts telling me that he wanted to reach out and hold me. Yet, I felt as though I barely knew the man. It was madness to feel like I belonged with these men, with Tommy, but I did. No matter what rationality I tried to apply to it, I felt as though I'd known them for decades.

"Where's Tommy's mom?" I asked, taking the plate.

Gabe hesitated, his fingers tightening on the dish. "What did Hudson say when you asked him?"

Something sensitive, then. I shrugged and picked up the sandwich instead, taking a bite of it. Gabe would break for me in a moment or two, I had no doubt. He was too interested in what I wanted, in keeping me happy. I could practically smell it on him, even with my lacking human nose.

"I don't know if it's my place," he said.

I finished the sandwich in two bites, starving. No wonder the wolves at the zoo paced, always looking for food, if they were as hollow as I was. "Did she leave him or something?"

"She died when Tommy was only a few months old," Gabe said, sitting down on the bed beside me.

Oh, no. "I'm so sorry."

"You didn't know," he said. "Becca was all sunshine and rainbows, but when she had her paws under her it was a different story. She and Hudson had gotten a taste for lamb, fresh and raw, during her pregnancy. It was a stupid thing, absolutely reckless. But their blood was up and she was in heat, and alphas will do anything for an omega in heat."

I frowned at him. "In heat. You're serious."

"You'll come into heat, too. Probably next moon cycle. Most omegas do, and that's something we all need to talk about. Because if you're out running around by yourself, you're likely to end up with some strange alpha trying to breed you. We can help prevent that."

The thought of some random wolf trying to do that to me was horrible. I shook my head at the idea of it, but Gabe smirked. "They all deny it when they're human, but a wolf in heat has only a few motivations. And they all do it."

"And you're any better? What do you... alphas, right?" I asked.

"Right."

I nodded. "You alphas, you're any better than us? You just said that Hudson did reckless, stupid things for this Becca because she was in heat."

"It wasn't just because of that. They'd been together for a few years and he was a party animal around her. It didn't matter what it was, if she got it into her head, he was all for it. And when lamb from the store wasn't doing it for her anymore, we bought the property out in the sticks and started hunting."

I frowned, some memory tugging at my mind. "This wasn't about five years back, was it?"

"Yeah. It was. And the sheep farm thing was about three years ago."

Though I'd helped to clean up my neighbor's farm after the slaughter of six market lambs in a night, I hadn't thought anything of it. The livestock guardian dog had been getting on in years and no one had blamed him for missing a few lambs in a pen when he was out with the rest of the flock, half a mile away.

But I'd been the one to say that the paw prints had been awfully big, that the destruction to the lambs had been almost surgical. It had been like the wolves; and they'd had to be wolves, the county agricultural board agreed with me, had known exactly where to strike to make the kills as painless as possible.

"It was you guys," I said, baffled.

Gabe shrugged. "We're predators, Sadie. They're soft prey animals without the defenses of the wild ones. Once we started, it was hard to stop. And if Becca hadn't been shot, I don't know that we ever would have."

"She was shot?" I breathed, my head turning toward Tommy's room.

He sighed. "The farmer caught us. He fired, we scattered. But Becca had blood on her paws from the kill and he found her in the woods. And he shot her. She fled into the night, but we found her the next morning. There was nothing we could do."

"But you called an ambulance anyway?" I asked.

"No."

"The hell do you mean by no? You just let her die?"

Gabe wrapped an arm around me and I stiffened against him. We were talking about a woman's death and he wanted to cuddle up to me? "She'd bled out by the time we found her. He hit an artery and no matter how fast you heal, a clipped artery takes you down pretty quickly. There was no reason to call an ambulance to deal with someone who had already passed. We buried her, informed her sister, and put out to the public that Hudson and she had broken up."

I relaxed against him, listening to him. "I'm sorry. I know she was Hudson's but I'm sure you two were close, too."

"She was mine, too."

"Is that some weird werewolf thing, too?"

That brought a smile back to Gabe's face. "Sometimes. Omegas aren't that common and alphas are everywhere. A lot of alphas form closely knit alpha-only packs and find a single omega. They share him or her and make them the king or queen of their universe. They're spoiled rotten and cared for all their days."

"I don't know if I need anybody to take care of me, exactly," I said, though I had to admit the idea of not worrying so much about where my next meal was coming from was appealing.

"Maybe that's a poor choice of words. It's more than just caretaking. It's helping. It's making sure that you have what you need for your rescue, watching your back, keeping rogue alphas away from you when you're in heat or when you're out hunting. It's bringing you back the choicest cuts of meat from a deer we run down." Gabe wrapped the other arm around me. I fit perfectly under his chin.

But it wasn't meant to last. Tommy gave a howl from his room and it broke my heart into a thousand pieces. I slid away from Gabe and wandered, almost like a person possessed, toward the child's room. The puppy's room? It didn't matter, the idea was merging into one and the same for me. I went to him as if I'd cared for him forever, pulled the lid off the crib; which I understood a great deal more now, and drew him into my arms.

And this time, he didn't bite me. He showed me his belly, his little paws flopping around. Then he rolled onto his side and looked at me, wanting something but I didn't know what. He looked plenty full of food, and my instincts said he didn't want down to go out. No, he wanted something from me, but what?

"He wants you to scent mark him," Xav said from the doorway.

I looked back at him. "I don't know how to do that."

"Come here."

My feet moved toward the big alpha before I realized what I was doing, which annoyed me. He pulled both of us into his arms and rubbed his chin across the top of my head, and oh.

Oh.

My legs went all wobbly, like I hadn't ever been touched by a man in my life. I was 14 again, kissing boys behind the school during our sophomore prom and not really knowing what to expect. The adrenaline left me breathless, but when I did inhale again it was that smokey campfire scent that rolled into my consciousness.

And it was so much more than that. Not only had I been marked, I felt as though I meant more to him. That he'd given me part of himself, somehow, and that meant a lot to the part of my mind that desperately wanted to go sink my teeth into another sandwich.

Tommy sniffed my cheek, his little nose cold. I tipped my head to the side and, far clumsier than Xavion, rubbed my scent on the pup. He responded by wiggling like a worm, nearly falling out of my arms twice before I got a proper hold on him. He shoved the top of his head against my jawline once, twice, then settled against me and immediately fell back to sleep.

"I have to wonder," Xavion said, "If he bit you because he wants you to be his mom."

There was a pregnant pause and I looked back at Xavion; well, back and up. He cleared his throat. "I'm not... implying anything, but he seems to be attached to you. And werewolf pups are picky."

"Is it weird if I feel so at home already?" I asked, setting my teeth on edge. "Especially after I was so stressed out just a little bit ago?"

What if he said yes? What if he thought I was being crazy? They had tons of money, more than I'd ever have. I was sure that they expected me to drop a lawsuit over Tommy's bite but, how could I? The only way the place could feel more like home was if Hudson came back with Bosco and the others.

I wasn't the best at being forward with other people. It wasn't hard for me to teach a dog how to be polite, wave their paw, or ask for a treat. But when it came to other folks, outside of pet-related neglect, I just wasn't some steel pillar with a silver tongue. I was just me, Sadie Faye, looking for friends on the internet when I didn't have anything else to do.

"It's not weird."

His voice was a rumble, almost a purr, in his chest. I leaned back into it, closing my eyes and nestling up against his chin again. I wanted more of his woodsmoke on me, wanted to feel Hudson's lips on my neck, Gabe's hands running down my sides. Was this part of being in heat? Would that start earlier than the full moon?

I was so full of questions, but I couldn't seem to get them all out. Besides that, there were some things a lady needed to ask another girl. Like, was the heat just the sort of thing that dogs experienced? Was it a period? Would I act like the goats up the road who yelled and rubbed their junk along the fence until a buck came and took care of that for them?

Because I was pretty certain I didn't want to lay against a fence, baahing at the top of my lungs, and waggling my ass in the air.

Tommy snored softly, one little hind paw kicking at my chest. I tucked him back into his bed and locked the top once again. It wouldn't do for him to go run off somewhere or sneak away. Maybe I could spare a crate when we went out as a... a pack?

Were we a pack?

Xav trapped me once again, his head coming to rest behind mine. He drew my hips against his and I gave no resistance. There was a certain hardness against the back of my leg that made me catch my breath. "Are you sure you're a werewolf?"

He hmm'd at me and nipped the skin just below my ear in response.

I quivered like a leaf in a hurricane. "Because you're hung like a horse."

My voice came out as a whisper. Some part of me said that things were moving too fast, but the rest of me rebelled against it. I'd known these men since the dawn of time, could trust them with anything. They were caring for my animals, caring for me, and I them. Every instinct said that we belonged together.

We always had.

Xavion laughed, picked me up as if I weighed nothing, and carried me back off to my room. I lifted my arms to drape around his neck and tipped my head up, trying to kiss him. If Hudson had tasted like fine wine and select olives, I wanted to see if Xav was different. He had to turn slightly to get us both into the room and I missed, my lips falling on his cheek instead.

What a disappointment. Frustrated, I tried to capture him again. He tipped his head to the side and looked past me, smirking. Was that the game he wanted to play, then? I growled at him, my best impression of a displeased dog, and he laughed again.

"If you ask nicely, I'll let you. Omegas have to know where they stand," he said, tossing me onto the bed without a care in the world.

I landed on the mattress but I wasn't alone for very long. He kicked off his shoes and stalked me, the irises of his eyes lightening until they became a wolf's amber. I reached up for his tie and wrapped it around my hand, pulling him on top of me. "Please?"

"Please, what?" he asked, his voice rough in my ears.

He followed the tie as I lifted my lips to his, pressing into the kiss. The instinctual part of me that wouldn't shut up sighed with relief, turned around three times, and quieted down. I let go of the tie and deepened it, tasting his tongue and winding my own against his. The hunt, the kill, and under it, an addictive dose of nicotine that reminded me of years long past.

I hadn't had a cigarette in ages, but no former addict fully gets past the want for them. That desire tugged at me, a memory of spoiling myself on the name-brand thins, not the cheap stuff, when money was good. I arched into him as he slid his hands up my back and dragged his nails back down.

Quivering, I drew back from his lips and let my head fall back onto the pillows. He was there immediately, too-sharp canines sinking into my neck. I stilled, overwhelmed by the urgency in me to let him bite, rut, lock my body to his and-

Did werewolves have knots? The other canids I'd dealt with did. The image of him slamming something the size of a grapefruit into my body was something I'd never considered, but it made a little moan escape my throat.

In answer, the teeth dug deeper. My breath came in a short, trembling sigh and the tension in my bra released as he unsnapped it. My breasts fell heavily to my chest, still resting in their satin cups as those mischievous hands withdrew, pulled around me, and moved to take them from beneath my shirt.

Xavion left the straps on my arms, twisting the front of the bra with one hand to pull my forearms tight against my sides. He reached for my left breast with the roughened pads of his fingers, raked one across a pert nipple that left me moaning and bucking my hips into his, insistent, begging-

"Do you mind if someone else joins the party?"

Gabe sat down on the edge of the bed. Xavion stiffened, his lip curling at the other alpha. Swamped with lust, my mind foggy, I stared at Gabe through half-lidded eyes and smiled. "Three's my lucky number."

"Perfect."

Xavion eyed me for a moment, then scooted slightly to the side. He didn't leave me open to Gabe, but he did allow the other alpha to join us, sharing me between them. Gabe slipped beneath me, pulling me into his lap, and wrapping his hand in my hair. Though he was gentle, he used that handhold to turn my head to the side and kiss the pink marks Xavion had left from his bite.

"Jealous?" Xav asked, peeling the bra from under my shirt and discarding it on the ground.

His palms cupped my breasts, squeezing, rolling the nipples, massaging. I let out a helpless whimper and writhed on Gabe's lap, my hands dropping to my waistband. Slowly, my fingers disappeared beneath it, intent on the glorious wetness below.

Gabe snorted. "Of course." Then he followed the length of my arm down to my fly and gently swatted my hands away. "Let me, sweetheart."

It was Gabe's teeth that bit into my neck this time. I moaned again, offering him all the skin he wanted and submitting entirely. As Xavion nipped my ear, Gabe's fingers replaced my own and sunk deep into my entrance, two at once, all the way up to the bottom knuckle. His thumb found my clit and ran across it.

I stiffened, strangling a cry in my throat. I couldn't wake the puppy, no matter what they did to me. He was so peaceful, so sweet when he was asleep, but the building pressure in my lower belly was like a boiler. Heat ran from my knees and up my thighs, stoking the wonderful burning deep within.

Xavion never stopped. Gabe thrust inside me, out, then over once more. He concentrated on my clit, sending a shockwave of pleasure through me every time he touched me. The fingers inside crept higher and higher, his cock grinding into my ass as he helped me ride toward my release. I reached out for Xavion's groin, ground my palms into his hardness, and shifted back against Gabe with everything I had.

"Please," I whispered, looking up at Xavion.

He got the message. Withdrawing one hand, he cupped my chin and dragged me up into another kiss. Gabe's soft thumb pad rolled around my clit once, twice, and fireworks exploded across my senses. I moaned against Xav's lips, a piteous thing that pleaded for more, and I knew, beyond a doubt, that I was home.

Chapter 8
Hudson

Despite everything else that was wrong in my life, there was always Safeway.

When I'd been young, it had been the thing I looked forward to most. It was the only time my parents and I had always been together due to their busy work schedules. We'd taken Sundays off and gone to the grocery store together. Of course, it'd become a necessity when Mom had gotten weaker, older, and needed help carrying cans of soda into the house.

We hadn't known that she'd been sick, then. That my family was going to be ruined from the inside out. It was why I kept my pack so close even now. If something was going wrong, I wanted to be on top of it immediately.

Because if we had, maybe we'd been able to save her a lot of pain and suffering.

I walked up to the store, grabbed a cart, and headed inside.

How many billionaires do their own shopping? More than you might imagine. I wandered through the aisles, picking up this and that. We were low on so much stuff back at the house. I really needed to hire someone to keep stock of what we had, or maybe set up a spreadsheet myself.

The longer I took to get to the meat department, the better. I knew it was where she'd be, knew that she was waiting for me. If I arrived with a cart full of groceries, I looked like a responsible father; right? Of course, she'd wanted to see Tommy in person and that wasn't going to happen. The boy would smell like Sadie through the next few moon cycles and I was relieved that Lillian was banned from our hunting grounds.

That didn't mean that she didn't have other ways of finding him.

I shuddered and turned toward the back of the Safeway. My wolf noted that the beef really wasn't beef, but low-grade bison pretending. The ground chicken had some turkey filler in it as well as a little soy. The lamb looked good, smelled good. I was taken by the rich, dark meat, the idea of putting my paws against the bone and sinking my teeth into the muscle, tearing it away, listening to the dog on the porch snarl at us and-

No, that was what had led us here, wasn't it? Easy, Hudson.

"It took you long enough," Lillian snapped. "Where is my nephew?"

She stood a few feet from me, her body rigid. Lillian wore her civilian clothes, a sweater and a pair of slacks that made her look like a principal instead of a nun. Like me, she had a pile of food in her cart. I noted that she hadn't been able to resist the lamb and, upon seeing it, put it out of my mind. Whatever she wanted, I didn't.

"He's at the house, Lil," I said. "I'm not bringing him out into the cold for the hell of it."

Narrowing her eyes at me, she crossed herself. I arched a brow and sniffed the air for effect. "Should I pull a fire alarm? I smell smoke."

"Don't be such an arrogant ass," she snapped. "What happened?"

There was something softer in her voice in the question. I ignored it. She was made of steel that hadn't yet seen a die grinder. All sharp edges and burrs, Lillian wanted nothing more than to trap me in my own words. Maybe she was even using a recorder. We did live in a single-party state, after all.

"Nothing happened. Why would I bring a toddler out into a cold, wintery day if I don't have to? I don't know why you're being so crazy about this. He's at home, fast asleep."

"I have a right to see my nephew when I want to, Fontaine."

I rolled my eyes, which slowly traveled back toward the lamb. Resist, Hudson. The normies wouldn't like it if you started gnawing on a haunch in public. "Then call my secretary and make an appointment. Or come to the house on his birthday. You don't make the effort. That's not my fault and it damned sure isn't my responsibility to try to force my -son- on you."

"Look at you," she hissed, quieting so only I could hear her. "You're practically feral. You can barely keep your eyes off the display case. This is what got Becca dead. This and the sheer loneliness you left her in when you decided to start that stupid dog food company."

Called out, I glared back at her. "She made her own decisions. We both did. They were bad ones, Lil. Besides, I don't remember you complaining when your fur was covered in sheep's blood and you had wool between your teeth."

"And the dog food? God save us all, you only do it so you can breathe the livestock before they're slaughtered, probably bathe in their blood when it's gathered off the abattoir floor-"

"Give me a break," I said, leaning against my cart. "I've got more control than that. Tommy, though. He loves it when we have pork blood night. You know. A little hail Satan, a good crimson bath. Wholesome."

The effect was immediate. It was like setting her hair on fire. The crimson built from her neck, beneath that awful pink sweater, and slowly climbed until her entire face had darkened. I worked not to smile at her. It was hard.

But she had plenty to say to me, anyway. "You're trash. Do you know that? I don't care how much money you have, how much power you have. That's all human garbage. It doesn't matter to people like us."

"Keep your voice down," I snarled, my hand tightening on the mesh of the cart.

There was an odd grinding sound and I looked down to see the mesh fold in on itself. I sighed, pulled my hand free, and tried to act as though I hadn't just given it a new access hole.

She walked up to me and jabbed me in the chest with her finger. It hurt. "One of these days, we aren't going to have to keep our voices down about intra-pack relations. And until then, it isn't their world that rules us. It's ours, Hudson. And I'm calling a Meet at the next Moon to figure out what to do with a reckless mutt like you. When it's all said and done? I'll have my nephew where he belongs."

I reached for her throat but she skipped away, glaring at me. "Soon."

Lillian snatched her cart and lifted her nose in the air, walking away from me and my broken buggy. I chewed the inside of my cheek, trying to think through the problems presented. One, Tommy would be in trouble if she actually called a Meet. The local supernatural community would be livid with me for letting my son wander off and turn a human being.

Two, if Lillian took my son from me, I'd have very little left. Sure, I'd have the company and my pack, but taking a boy from his father is one of the cruelest things you can do to either of them. But werewolf fathers were supposed to be responsible for the actions of their children, especially the boys. It was archaic and probably had its roots in some sexist, long-forgotten child-raising theory, but the supernatural world was slower to change than the human world.

There were more risks in changing, too. When you tried to convince creatures that went bump in the night that they should concentrate their efforts on finding more progressive activities to do with their time, they usually tried to rebuke you by taking ten pounds of flesh out of your ass.

Last, and perhaps the one that grated me in an even more frustrating way than potentially losing my son, was Sadie. She would be killed to keep our lives and our identities a secret. They would never trust a freshly turned werewolf with no prior allegiance to keeping our secrets well... secret. She could try to talk her way out of it, try to charm them, but at the end of the day? The Meet would send the dragons to do their wet work for them. And there wasn't anything that I could do about it.

That was, unless I could convince them that she'd known about us. Perhaps I'd been intending to turn her and my son had simply misunderstood and gotten there first. Yes, I'd be in trouble for sneaking past the decorum and the paperwork for it. There was that tried and true method for turning someone.

But my getting in trouble for something like that was less likely to end with Sadie dead and, maybe, Tommy, too.

As I checked myself out at the self-check, I worked through the problems with that resolution. The largest, perhaps, was that I may be banished from the area. Gabe, Leo, and Xavion would take care of Tommy until I could scout a new place, re-settle us, and they could move to be with me. Sadie? I didn't know. She had the rescue to deal with and moving would completely destroy her as a resource for her community.

"You've got a whole heap of trouble in your face, boss," drawled a voice behind me.

I looked back at the familiar man who adjusted his glasses at me. His forest green eyes were amused. I knew for a fact that he'd broken his face a few times before he'd joined my pack, but I turned to wrap my arms around him anyway. "Leo. Aren't you supposed to be in warehouse?"

"Got out early. Seems that the more I do this, the better we get at beating your expectations," he said, patting me on the back. "You want a hand with all this?"

Most of what I'd scanned was bagged, but I waved him on anyway. "I won't complain. Saw Lillian a minute ago."

"You two meet up to talk about something?"

I raised my brows at him. "Something."

Either he got the message or he was smart enough to know I didn't want to talk about it in public. I was only warning him that she may still be lurking around, that he might have to deal with her, too. No one wanted to do that. Not even her sister had wanted to deal with her occasional hysterics, but she had.

There was a brief pang in my stomach when I thought of my mate. She'd been everything good in life, but our actions had gotten her killed. It'd been a stupid thing, a senseless thing, what we'd been doing to those sheep. Even knowing that death awaited at that ranch, it was hard not to go back and do it all over again.

A wolf doesn't really understand weapons. They understand pain and they understand hunting. A deer has antlers that can stab you, perhaps even break off under your skin and lead to infection. This is the way a human considers an interaction with a deer.

Not a wolf. To me, in my fur, a deer was simply a pointy steak. There was a chance that the deer might hurt me, but it was a chance I was willing to take. Yet, when it came to the sheep? Sure, some of them had horns. There were breeds that specialized in creating perfect specimens, big rams with huge curling horns that made them look stout and terrifying.

Yet, when we wolves approached, it hardly mattered. They ran along with the rest, screaming for their farmer to do something, anything, that would save them from the fury of our claws, our teeth. And there was little that those soft humans could do against our power, either.

I'd never taken the life of a human, finding myself to be a little too human still to do that. After all, the tears I'd shed for my mate were not something that a wolf was capable of.

"I'll see you at the house?" Leo asked, his voice apprehensive.

He'd stacked everything back in the cart. I grabbed the handle and nodded at him without another word. Something that was impossible to put a name to passed between us, a deeper sort of reassurance, and I headed back out toward my car.

Alphas seem to have an interpersonal bond that is very nearly telepathy. Maybe it's subtle body language, a way of communicating that we don't understand as humans but our wolves do, regardless of not being in control. I don't know and I'm hard put to explain it better than that. The thing is, we know.

Leo knew that I was upset, that something major had gone down. He probably assumed it was a threat. I tossed the groceries in the back of my car, smacked the trunk down, and returned the cart. It didn't hurt to be polite.

I assumed that Leo also knew I was worried. That would be enough to worry him, too. When the lead wolf of a pack is nervous, so is every other wolf around them.

Had I seen an officer on the way home, I have no doubt I would have been locked up for the evening. Though, occasionally, people of my status were overlooked, few cops were going to ignore 160 in a 45, regardless of my wealth or my power. It took me less time to get back to the house than it had getting there, but it was still a little over half an hour.

When I walked in, I saw not a scrap of the rest of my pack. No Gabe, no Xavion, no Sa-

No Tommy.

Yet, the door hadn't been smashed open. There was no unfamiliar pack scent hanging in the air, no brimstone and sulfur of the dragon shifters endemic to our region. I frowned and lifted my head toward the stairs, catching something that smelled of peaches and cream, of caramel and vanilla. It was sweet, savory, and landed on my tongue as much as it caught my nose by surprise. Feminine, gentle, but familiar.

But not. Different, but comforting. Again, familiar, but new. I gave my head a shake, trying to narrow it down. Confused, I followed it and the heady aroma of my packmates. It wasn't until I got to the second floor landing the arousal, almost the exact scent of Old Spice, touched the rest of it.

I scowled. I'd told them to take care of her, not fuck her. God damn it. I stalked toward the nearest door and shoved it open, yet no one was there. The entire floor was thick with the smell of sex, a bitch nearly in heat and ready to present to every mutt who would knot with her. I'd been an idiot, not ordering them to leave her alone. Gabe and Xavion were notorious when it came to the ladies and, sometimes, the beta males, too.

I opened another door and found nothing but an empty bed. It was the third room that I was lucky with. There, wrapped in the sheets and squirming back against Xavion's groin, was Sadie. Her face was flushed, her tongue falling from her gasping mouth. My packmates worked their way over her naked body, though they remained clothed themselves. Along her neck were tiny, pink marks from their teeth.

Though, I noted, that no one had actually put a claim on her. An alpha's bite would mark an omega forever, bonding the two of them as if they were one. It would work with multiple alphas, were they joined in a pack as we were, but usually the lead wolf went first.

And that meant she was *mine*.

It was a beautiful scene, watching her undulate pinned between my pack brothers. Gabe drew her nipple into his mouth and she wrapped her fingers in his hair. Xavion lifted her from the bed, slid beneath her, and licked his lips as he readied himself to slurp her creamy center down to the last.

That was when I cleared my throat and the room went still. I walked to the closet, found a comfortable robe, and moved to the bedside. I offered it out to her wordlessly.

Xavion and Gabe withdrew as one, Xavion amused, Gabe guilty. I didn't bother to look at them. They hadn't disobeyed an order, hadn't done anything that I wouldn't have done before I'd mated myself to someone and become a father. Sex was taboo for humans, not for us.

You took what pleasure you could in an otherwise fucked up world.

Sadie still panted, though she took the robe. I watched as it slid over her shoulders, wrapped around all that wonderful, bare skin and hid it from view again. Had the matter not been pressing, had I not made up my mind in the car, perhaps I would have joined. Or, more likely, I would have slipped out of the room once more and allowed them to continue their play until they were tired of it.

But there were pressing matters to discuss. There were problems to attend to. And that meant that forcing her to her hands and knees, knotting her, making her howl?

Backburner.

And goddamn did I regret that.

"Did I do something wrong?" she asked, her voice dreamy and breathless.

I ran my hand through her hair, damp and messy though it was. "I should have warned you. I apologize. We need to take you somewhere. Do you trust us to do that?"

"I trust you."

She didn't meet my eyes when she said it, instead focusing on my chest. My fingers stopped in her hair as she leaned against me. Heart thundering, I combed it through one last time and looked up at Gabe. "Let's get ready for a camping trip."

Chapter 9
Sadie

I'd never been in one of those giant extended Hummer trucks before.

Hudson drove. Gabe played navigator. Xavion snored in the trunk area, stretched out and kicked back. Tommy was fast asleep in his car seat, bafflingly human and looking so much like his dad, midway through the vehicle. But me? I had the entire back seat to myself.

And it was lonely.

Though I'd been able to dress myself before we left, I'd completely forgotten how to fasten a bra. We left it behind with the excuse that no one would care if I were naked in the middle of the woods, much less braless.

Unfortunately, the fog was beginning to clear from my mind. I missed my dogs, though I was certain that they were being well cared for. I missed my house, though there was a place where the roof leaked and the carpet was worn. And I missed my car, hunk of junk that it was, because it was mine.

I felt as though I were whining for no good reason. My God, I'd been in a mansion with finery that I couldn't dream of. Yet all I wanted was to go back home, taking Tommy and my new packmates along with me. Did werewolves den? Was that what I was feeling? So many questions and I only had the men around me as a resource.

Given that the internet was some sort of bastion for curiosities, I was sure that if I went looking I'd probably find both real werewolves and the fake sorts that wear Hot Topic gear and howl at the moon outside the mall on Friday nights. And hey, I'd been one of those, too. Vampires had been my thing, not werewolves, but the Venn diagram overlapped enough between the two groups that it may as well have been a single circle.

The Hummer was great at off-roading, bouncing us but not throwing me out of my seat. I hadn't expected it to handle the rough terrain, but then, they were a luxury vehicle and most of those were decent at it. Did the rich and famous spend their time jumping all over the woods, rolling through lush undergrowth and heading out to personal wilderness cabins?

It was what the commercials made you believe, and it damned sure was what me and my new pack were doing.

I paused on that for a moment. My new pack? Is that what they were? We hadn't made any kind of promise to one another, no undying love or whatever werewolves did. I ran over the potential in my mind and tried it out loud. "My new pack."

"Yes?" Hudson asked.

The heat crept up my neck. "I was just trying it out, that's all."

"Whatever happens, no matter what they decide, it's true. Do you understand that?"

It climbed further, darkening my cheeks as I turned to look out the window. I didn't answer, not yet. I didn't really understand. Just because they were my pack, were they able to protect me from whatever was coming? Is that why we were out in the middle of nowhere? It wasn't like I was judging. I'd spent most of my life in the middle of nowhere and I loved it, despite the comforts of civilization being a long drive.

The thing was, it was a pretty drive. I watched the trees as we drove past them, their colors long since shed. What had been a miracle, avoiding the snow the other night, had come to fruition since I'd left home. Snow lay everywhere, the roads freshly salted. I assumed it was by those who lived in the area, because I really doubted that the local authorities came out and did it so quickly.

"We might be stuck out here if it snows like this again," I called to the front seat.

Hudson didn't respond. He turned down a trail that hadn't been cared for whatsoever. The Hummer easily peeled through the snow, leaving tracks in our wake. It was Gabe who spoke to me. "We're prepared for that. Plenty of wood, tons of food, and there's good hunting this far out. We'll be safe."

"Once you get back," Hudson said.

Gabe shrugged. "Once Xav and I get back. Leo's supposed to be here in the next hour or two, too."

I'd almost forgotten the invisible part of their pack. It wasn't as if I'd heard much about him, but the idea of another alpha to ...well.

That blush reappeared on my cheeks and I swallowed, looking out the window once again. This wasn't the time or the place to relive the intensity Gabe, Xavion, and I had experienced back at the house. Even so, my thighs pressed together and I shivered.

"Have to get back pretty fast," Xav whispered in my ear from the trunk. "Smells like you need all your alphas."

I looked back at him, keeping my voice low, too. "Is it normal for you guys to share like this?"

"Natural, really. Packs share everything."

"I'm an every*one* not an every*thing*."

He grinned at me and disappeared behind the seat again. "You can be both."

We stopped suddenly enough that the Hummer jerked. Tommy was startled awake and started to fuss. I hurried forward to shush him and get him out of that chair. When I'd been a kid, I'd ridden everywhere on my mom's lap. I knew it wasn't the safest thing, but having him all strapped down and away from me just...

I don't know. It did something that was probably completely illogical. Hudson opened the door and helped the two of us out.

Before me stood a log palace the size of one of those hunting lodges you see way up north. I'd been expecting a hovel, maybe two rooms and an outhouse. I'd thought I'd be cooking by candlelight. Instead, Gabe ran around back and, I assumed, turned on a generator or something. The house was suddenly awash in amber light, glowing with warmth among all that frosty white.

Tommy made a sound in my arms and I didn't hesitate. I took him straight inside and wrapped both of us in a pile of blankets. A heater kicked on and blew toasty air through the ceiling vents, though I assumed that such a large cabin would take a while to heat.

I heard the Hummer crunch away once more as Hudson came up behind us, carrying wood, newspapers, and a book of matches. He walked to the fireplace, settled the wood and newspapers, then came back to the couch Tommy and I had crashed on. He kissed the top of my head, grabbed the back of the couch, and pushed the two of us over in front of the fireplace.

Then, he crouched and struck a match.

A breath of wind from the fireplace blew it out.

He eyed the book of matches, which stated that they were wind-resistant, and struck another. I leaned forward and whispered, "Woosh."

That one, too, blew out. I smiled back at Tommy as he laughed. Hudson snorted at both of us and struck a third. Tommy was too excited. Like most little kids, he really hadn't mastered the idea of blowing yet. Instead, he yelled and spit at the match at the top of his lungs.

And it, too, extinguished in Hudson's hand.

I smiled, hiding it beneath my blanket. Pulling the little guy back, I snuggled him close. He nestled into me readily, his father's bold, dark eyes crinkling at the edges in just the same way. "Let your dad go on and light a fire."

"Daddy makes good fires."

His tiny voice melted me, like a marshmallow dropped in a campfire. I beamed at him. "I bet he does. Your daddy's probably very good with his hands."

Another match was struck, fumbled, but it fell into the paper. Hudson cleared his throat and blew into the flames. The embers scattered, but the flame flickered to life among the tinder. As it caught, he stacked a few smaller sticks, then a couple of split logs on the rungs above the tiny fire.

Was he blushing? I grinned at him as he faced me, a tint of red in his cheeks. I patted the cushion beside us. "Always room for more."

"I think it's time Tommy had his nap," Hudson said, directing a look at his son.

Of course, the boy whined at him. Who wants to take a nap when you're in an exciting new place? Well, maybe not so new for him, but certainly for me. I hugged him and mock-whispered, loud enough that Hudson could hear, "Maybe if you're very good and take a quick nap, we can have ice cream when you get up."

Tommy's eyes lit with excitement. He pulled the blanket off of me, which I was careful to let go of, and marched right off down the hallway. It was bigger than he was, dragging behind him like a superhero cape. Hudson followed him dutifully and I watched as the first log began to snap and pop.

It reminded me of being little at my grandparents' house, the place I now owned. I hoped that whoever was caring for my rescues was making certain the heat worked. Every now and then it would go on the fritz, making me spend money that I didn't have; but I couldn't let a sweet old lady like Carrie Ann freeze.

Mind you, she was the sort that'd just weasel her way into bed with you whether she was cold or not; didn't matter if the heat was blasting or if it was the dead of summer. She was a snuggler and you were in her way. I'd woken up more than once with a big paw whacking me in the face.

So, you know. I put my hand back over her snout. That's how you work with animals like her; you meet them at their level. She'd snort, I'd snort. She'd groan and shove me further off the bed. I'd laugh and pull her with me. She was a good girl.

"You have a real way with kids," Hudson said.

I jumped and looked back at him, tilting my head. "Same theory as dealing with the critters. You just have to convince them to make the right decisions."

"Yeah?" He tilted his head at me. "So what's the right decision now?"

My heart sped up and it was suddenly noteworthy that he'd banished the other two wolves back to work and left himself with me. Alone.

Especially after what he'd walked in on at their mansion.

"I'm..." I started, but I didn't know what else came after that word. I'm what?

He sat down beside me, elegant, strong, and foreboding. His fingers brushed across my cheek and he leaned forward, drawing me in. Our lips met and fire exploded inside of me, licking its way through my body and sending gooseflesh out along my arms and thighs. The room was nowhere near as cold as it had been, though it had everything to do with the flames within and nothing to do with the logs popping to life beside us.

God, he tasted like cheat day on the strictest diet you can imagine. Maybe Tommy hadn't really needed a nap, not after the trip, but we needed him to have one. And sometimes, when you're a parent, that happens.

Hudson bore me to the cushions and I pulled him to me, my arms around his neck, fingers rolling over the thick muscles in his shoulders. We broke apart only to breathe, then collapsed together again. My instincts howled for him to take me, for me to roll onto my belly and arch my back, to beg him to pin me down. It was so strange, so wild, that I broke our third-ever kiss and blinked up at him.

"Teach me what to do to make the wolf happy," I whispered, pleading.

A chuckle came from deep in his chest. "I'd be happy to."

He ran the tip of his index finger along my neck and stopped at the hollow of my throat. His lips followed the line a moment later and my eyes rolled back in my head. I wanted him and Gabe and Xav and a big, warm den to hide our treasures in. I wanted rich, red meat every night and rough, screaming sex every morning. I wanted to let the mansion burn and to stay out here in the woods where they could throw me down in a pile of leaves, or even put me on my knees in the frost, where no one could hear me crying their names, one right after the other.

If men get blue balls, we ladies must get something similar. Swamp syndrome, maybe? I don't know what to call it, but I needed him inside of me, hard and thick, plowing away all the bad times and planting good ones. I needed him to drive his knot into me and stay there, forever on top of me, protecting me, promising me that he'd never-

That they'd never leave.

That I'd never be alone again.

Was it wrong to beg for permanence when the world didn't work like that?

Hudson rolled my shirt collar to the side and lowered his head to sink his teeth into the nape of my neck. I lifted my head to press it against him, willing him to understand the comfort, the satisfaction, that he brought to my new feral side. I didn't know if it worked or not, but he trailed his hands further south, unbuckling my belt and tossing it to the floor beside us.

I tried to reciprocate but he growled, using his grip on my jeans to press me deeper into the couch. I submitted in an instant, never even thinking about it, and hung back. Pleased, he peeled my pants and panties from me as one, leaving them attached at the ankles.

The bite was short-lived. I whined at him, but he narrowed his eyes at me. "Do you want a real bite? A mark that never fades?"

"*Yes*," I sighed, squirming my arm from my shirt. It left me half exposed to him, but he seemed to appreciate the view.

He licked his lips and moved back from me, patting my thigh. "Roll over. Get up on your knees. If you want the full omega experience, I'll give it to you."

Everything in me lit up. Though his voice had a touch of a warning, I ignored it. I was on my belly, shoving myself up onto my hands and knees. He let out a quivering sigh and ran his hands over my ass. I tipped my head back and leaned into his palms, my empty core aching for fulfillment.

"Last chance," he said, his thumb running over my slit and opening me just enough. A droplet of me ran down his wrist. I only knew because I heard him lick it off.

In answer, I slid a hand beneath myself and reached for his groin. If he wasn't going to get those slacks off, I would.

There was the slightest pause. Those severely creased slacks ended up on the ground with my belt, though he left his shirt on. His fingers reached forward and twisted in my hair, using it for leverage. My tongue fell from my mouth, as if I'd run miles on paws I didn't have.

And then, nirvana.

He hilted his cock in me in a slow, single movement. I felt every inch force its way into me, stretching me, filling me entirely. And at the end, the slightest bulge of a knot promising something I knew nothing about.

Yet.

But God, I wanted to learn. I let out a soft groan as he drew back, plunged into me again, then pulled away once more. Each thrust left me helpless, putty in his hands, pleading to be shaped into something new. A brave thing, fierce and strong, soft and protective. He pulled my head back by my hair, the pain lacing its way into the pleasure to give me new insight on the manner in which I'd ever considered either of them.

His hot breath dampened the back of my neck. Claws came up, sharp tips digging into my breast as he quickened, each crushing of his hips into mine, ending in a pant that promised more delicious violence. I reveled in it, transformed beneath it, and- whoops, transformed a little too much. Fluffy dark fur spread along my right arm, distracting me until sharpened canines snapped into the exact same spot he'd bitten before.

I dropped my weight forward and Hudson followed me, the couch devouring us as a hot trickle slid down my neck. His tongue ran over the bite and I felt him behind me, knew he felt me, too. His knot hit me once, twice, and popped into me with a slick, hot noise that blinded me to anything but the two of us.

And I knew, without asking, that he felt the same.

Hudson rutted into me, his knot locking us together and forcing his thrusts in short, staccato time that left me breathless. He conquered me, claimed me, fucked me into the couch until I could barely think. His mark burned on my neck, my claws shredded the armrest in front of me, and I choked on a moan as my belly muscles tightened, my climax covering everything else in a wave of ecstasy.

Warmth filled me, shot after shot, as I slowly came back to reality. Hudson's arms were wrapped tight around me, his cock pulsing as he unleashed his load. He turned us to one side and a bit of armrest fluff fell onto my head, but I was certain he could replace the damned couch any time he wanted.

When he was finished, he drew his teeth away from me and simply held me. I turned my head to nestle my new mate, to bathe in his scent and his sweat, to taste my blood in his mouth.

And it was perfect.

Which meant it couldn't last.

Chapter 10
Leo

I followed Lillian, but it didn't lead me to a greater understanding of why she was such a bitch.

Okay, joking aside, she'd had it out for all of us since the day Hudson had taken Becca as his mate. She'd only gotten worse since they'd had the pup and, with her sister out of the picture, she'd been treating Hudson like he was public enemy #1 for far too long.

So I followed her and maybe I watched her go inside her place. Maybe I let her see me. She knew who I was within the pack. If a threat had to be put down, Hudson rarely dirtied his hands with it. Instead, he asked me to see to it.

And I never let him down.

Let her come to her own conclusions, let her stew and peek out her windows at night. When the moon was dark, when Mother's eyes were closed and wolves settled things like wolves, instead of the cowardly human bodies we hid within; that was when she would expect me. She would tremble, ready herself like a prey animal.

Yet I wouldn't be there. It would break her mind, drive her to think about something else other than that bite.

Tommy had fucked up, but he was too young to really understand the problems he'd created. It wouldn't stop the Meet from killing him, Sadie, and maybe the rest of us. But maybe they'd be nice enough to do it from behind, to let him go down eating an ice cream cone when one of those dragon assholes blasted him with enough fire to ashify him instantly.

I'd only ever seen it done once, but that was two too many times for me.

After tailing Lillian for most of the afternoon, I headed out to the cabin with a car full of supplies. Fort Woof, as I personally called it, was several hundred acres of trees that the Fontaine Foundation (an off-shoot of Fontaine Feeds, of course) had purchased to keep hunters out and preserve the natural beauty of the world.

It was also the perfect place for a small pack of werewolves to enjoy themselves during full moon nights, to hunt what we wanted, and to give in to our true natures.

Maybe I was a little bit of an anarchist. No one expected the guy in the glasses to be fine with watching the world burn. No, it was always the spiky-haired, collared rebel that yelled at the establishment that wanted to set shit on fire and let it all go to hell. Yet those people were some of the most likely to try to uphold the status quo when push came to shove.

Personally? I was fine with putting the dragons in their place, dropping the whole secret supernatural community vibe, and eating a baby now and then. Baby sheep, baby deer, baby human; whatever. Munchie crunchies.

Which meant that without Hudson, I'd have probably been killed years ago. I was too risky, too wild to be allowed to survive when the entire supernatural world was terrified of humanity. They had a point. There were far more humans than there were any of us. Even if we banded together, we'd have been struck down in a several-tens-of-thousands-to-one conflict. And when I looked at my nephew playing innocently, I imagined all of us wiped out.

And let me tell you, it made me just sad enough not to go screw up that whole status quo.

Fuckin softie I am, let me tell you what.

The drive back to the cabin was a quiet one, with me only having to dodge some idiotic deer once. What we did on moonlit nights was population control, as necessary as the hunters that were allowed to clear out the woods during winter. Their season was upon us and I was ever more grateful for our sanctuary. Sure, trespassers were a possibility, but it was less likely to happen when we left big, wolfy pawprints all over the perimeter of our land.

Few hunters, however brave, wanted to screw around with wolves. That ratio I mentioned? It shrinks considerably when it's a pack of us against two or three of them in bright orange. We'd never had to kill before to protect ourselves, but there was a first time for everything.

I grabbed as many bags as I could carry, including two in my teeth, and nudged the cabin door open.

Her scent hit me full in the face and I wasn't ready for it.

Fur prickled to life on the back of my neck, down my spine, and along the tops of my ears. I inhaled and let it out with a shudder. The new girl was almost in heat and someone had barebacked her into next week. And, jealous as I was, I was deeply impressed by the fact that Hudson had let loose. The guy had been a stick since his mate had passed. He'd needed their romp as much as she did from the smell in the room.

I wandered into the kitchen and found Hudson, fully dressed and looking very pleased with himself, chopping jalapenos for dinner. A dozen steaks lay out on the counter, covered with a dry rub that he'd been using since we were all in college. Nutmeg, ginger, and a handful of other oddities went into it, but I swear, it was the best steak I'd ever tasted.

"Where are the others?"

I snorted and dumped the groceries on the counter. "Always nice to be appreciated. I bring you food, booze, take care of all the puppy dogs and kitty cats-"

"You didn't have to take it upon yourself, you know. And I did send a dozen helpers once you told me that it was an actual rescue, not some sort of miniature zoo," Hudson said, popping a knob of butter from one of the many sticks on the counter and tossing it into the pan.

I started to put the dry goods up, leaving the frozen shit to thaw. It always irritated him when I did that. "I'm just jealous that you got her before I did."

The first steak snapped and crackled as he smacked it into the pan. A bit of hot butter jumped onto my skin and I tightened my hands at the shock of pain. Slight, pleasant, threatening to make my pants tighter than they already were.

Hudson eyed me. "You're a real kinky fuck."

"Your cousin knows better than you ever will," I said, putting a box of cereal away.

"Right. But where are Gabe and Xav? They aren't answering the phone and I expected them to show up about the same time you did."

I crumpled the bag and stuffed it into another, as you do. "I didn't see them on the road. Could be that they were a little behind me and didn't have a signal. The weather's getting worse. Just means that Lillian won't run out here to fuck with us."

If I'd thrown a punch at him, Hudson wouldn't have been more surprised. He dropped the spatula and stared at me. "I didn't think of that."

"You really didn't think of the fact that Lil knows exactly where this place is? That she knows because we rented it all the time for full moons and she came along?"

He scowled at me. "She just knows we rented it. She has no idea that we bought the place and the land with it."

"It doesn't take a rocket scientist to put two and two together, Huds."

The spatula retrieved, he chucked it in the sink and pulled out another one. "I'm open to suggestions."

"We spend the night here, load back up, and head to her place. Lillian doesn't know who she is, and the Meet won't congregate until the full moon. Besides. There's stuff that needs to be fixed there and we could all use a break from corporate land."

I finished off the last of the groceries and watched him as he contemplated it. As he moved the first steak from the pan to a plate so it could rest, he sighed. "It makes you feel like less of a man to hide at a woman's house."

He wasn't wrong. A small part of me was perfectly happy to face the oncoming danger with claws and fangs, but that wouldn't serve Tommy or our new pack member. She was too new, too young, and had no idea what she was doing in a fight on her paws. I was sure she could throw a punch as a person, but the furious dance that was a wolf's fighting capability took years to learn.

We didn't have years to teach her.

"Let me talk to her," I said. "I'm sure she has a thousand questions and all you've done is put your dick in her. Where's she at?"

Hudson crinkled his nose at me. "You're so goddamned crass. Billions of dollars and you sound like some frat asshole."

"I make you cuss," I beamed. "That's what matters to me. Where is she?"

"Upstairs."

Perfect. I slapped him on the ass and trotted away. Up the stairs I went, following her scent. It was touched with bubble bath and freesia oil, though I had to admit I'd never seen a freesia flower so I had no idea if it was authentic or not. The walk was quick, I was surprisingly tired after my day, and I hoped I'd be able to sink my teeth into the steaks before Xav got a single bite.

Of the many doors on the hallway, only one was cracked open. Inside, I heard splashing. I certainly wasn't going to complain if I caught her getting out of the tub. I crept inside, the splashing increasing. Was she rolling around in there or something?

Rather than walking in on a gorgeous, by all the accounts I'd heard so far, young woman without so much as a single fur on her, I stepped in on an ice cream-covered Tommy happily sending water everywhere. Sadie finished cleaning his little hands and moved on to wiping off his face, murmuring to him as she worked.

"Unk Lee-oh!"

Well, Tommy recognized me. But Sadie didn't. She spun on her toes, her eyes changing color as she lunged. There was no pause to see if I was a relative or a friend, she only knew the pup was potentially in danger and that she was the only thing standing between him and whoever was behind her.

God, we'd needed someone like her for such a long time.

I caught her as she tackled me to the floor and rolled her onto her back, pinning her against the floor. "Pretty aggressive to the kid's uncle."

She stared up at me for a moment and then the instinct took over. Her head turned to the side, looking away from an alpha's intense gaze. A part of me was smug about it, reveling in the fact that she felt a need to submit even when the pup was in potential danger.

Then the human side kicked in and she gasped, pulling herself away from me. "I'm so sorry. Oh my gosh. You must be Leo. I'm so sorry, I didn't mean to do anything. I just didn't know you were there!"

"It's not the first time a woman's thrown herself at me, won't be the last," I grinned, forever the charmer.

She sighed at me. "Really?"

I widened my grin and, without looking, reached over to pluck Tommy out of the tub. Sure, he was still a little sticky, but what kid isn't? I wiped his face off with my sleeve and grabbed the towel nearby. "Always. But yeah, I'm Leo. Cat name, wolf mind, gorgeous body."

"I suppose it's good to meet the entire pack before I'm forcibly dragged away from all of you."

She sounded so defeated. As if we wouldn't be interceding on her behalf, or as if the rest of the world had already condemned her. They probably had, but it didn't mean that she had to know that. "The Meet will go as well as it can. You'll be safe and sound, and you won't have a worry in the world once it's over and done with."

"More like I won't remember any of this. Hudson said the dragons can change your mind and, after I got over the idea of friggin' dragons bein' a thing, just—" Sadie shook her head, taking Tommy and continuing to dry him off. "It ain't enough that there's werewolves. Now there's dragons and they're psychics. They probably run the whole fortune teller hotlines stuff."

"Far as I know, they got out of the business a while ago," I told her.

Sadie sighed at me again. "You aren't even kidding, are you?"

"I don't think I'd joke about something like that. Last I knew, they sold it off to the unicorns."

Her brows came together, uncertain if I was pulling her leg. Maybe I needed to be easier on her. She hadn't been raised around the things of folk tales and legends like the rest of us. We got Tommy dressed and let the little guy go scampering off to cause mayhem, like toddlers tend to do.

"It's all really confusing," she said, watching him run out the door. "I'm trying to understand it all, I really am, but so often I feel like I'm in some kind of dream. Or maybe a coma. Like, maybe I wrecked on the way home and nobody's kind enough to tell me."

I sat down on the edge of that room's bed and stretched out my legs, my knees stiff from driving. Fucking winter. "Why would you feel like that?"

"First some werewolf pup turns up, then I'm being all but gangbanged by three hot as hell guys with more power and money than I'll ever have-"

"It could be four if you wanted it," I offered.

Her personal scent flooded the room. A blush snuck up her cheeks and she couldn't hold eye contact with me. Tempted as I was, I didn't make another move on her. From the lower level's aroma, she needed a break and I wasn't about to make her squirm unnecessarily.

"But maybe another time," I said. "You're going to a Meet and you have no idea what's going to happen to you, do you?"

She shook her head. "Hudson's pretty determined for it to not happen in the first place. I appreciate that but I guess I broke some kind of rule...?"

I patted the bed beside me. She sat down and leaned against me. I could practically taste her. "When we decide to turn a human into one of us, there is a process. We start out by revealing what we are, talk to them about the problems they may face, and explain our society to them. You didn't get any of that because the kid bit you."

"Are you here to play teacher?"

Her voice was rich, warm, and promised a short, plaid skirt and a too-tight white shirt; the type that I could rip the buttons off of to get to the woman underneath. I eyed her and she gave me a wide, bright smile that was all sweet innocence. I prodded her right between the ribs and she jumped, laughed, and nestled back against my shoulder.

"One of these days, I'll use your pigtails like reins. But not right now. It's just... polite to let an omega rest after she bonds with an alpha. To let things settle in." I grinned. "But Gabe and Xav are going to be super jealous."

"Why would they know?"

"Because you can smell the two of you all over the house, especially as soon as you walk in." I told her and the color darkened in her cheeks. I shook my head. "It's not like that with us. Sex isn't taboo. It's... good. It's part of being pack. And it makes the pack bigger. There are all sorts of ceremonial rites that involve sex outside, under a full moon, to honor Mother and mothers in general."

She blinked up at me. "Mother?"

"The moon. She watches over us, cares for us. She gave us the power to be of Her kind, of paw and claw, fang and fur. I don't know if I'd call it worship so much as it's just werewolf culture. It's what we're raised with. It's so embedded in who we are that we don't really think twice about it."

"Like everyone referring to Christmas as a named day instead of December 25th."

I nodded. "Exactly like that."

She took a breath and held it, sighed, and ran her fingers absently over the pale pink scar on the side of her neck. I knew Hudson's bite well. I'd taken it a few times. It just didn't leave a mark on another alpha. "So, I need to talk about the moon and puppies and... what else? To prove to this Meet that I'm right for the pack?"

"It's probably better if you don't talk at all. Since we're the accused party, we'll do what we can to protect you. We don't get someone on the judgment staff because we'd be bias. They're shapeshifters, all of them. Dragon, griffin, unicorn, and one of the big cat shifters. They're likely to be in their animal bodies to try to frighten you. But we can prepare you for that."

There was steel in her gaze when she looked up at me. She nodded, chewed her upper lip with her bottom teeth, and tightened her hold on me. "Teach me everything I need to know. I'll do everything I can to stay with the pack. I know it sounds crazy but I feel like I belong here."

I pressed my forehead to hers and gave her a gentle, chaste kiss. "It doesn't sound crazy at all."

Chapter 11
Sadie

I spent the night in Hudson's arms. Leo slept in the same bed as us, but he wasn't much of a cuddler. It turned out that he preferred to sleep at the foot of the bed in the shape of a wolf, just in case anyone broke down the door or something.

After all, Gabe and Xavion had never turned back up.

They also weren't answering their phones, which was just as worrisome. Hudson had called Tommy's aunt, the one who had summoned the Meet in the first place, but to no avail. Leo had assured me that kidnapping wasn't a common issue in the supernatural community, even when the Fae were involved in disappearances. It was much more likely that Gabe and Xav had simply been caught in another dumping of snow.

My cell phone only got enough signal to show us that there was possibly some truth to it. After all, the weather radar showed snow in the general area of the city. They'd gone back to put things in order for my packmates to take the rest of the month off. Collectively, they wanted to teach me how things worked and the whys of their culture.

Beyond that, I think they wanted to be sure that I was real. These men, these incredible werewolves, could have had anyone they wanted.

But they wanted me. Just me, plain old Sadie. And sometimes, I had trouble believing that I wasn't in a dream.

I awoke just after dawn, expecting to find myself in my old bed and at the beck and call of someone who'd found opossums under their porch and needed help getting them out. That, or another person who'd come across an entire den of rattlesnakes in their shed for the winter. My answer to that call had been to seek professional snake assistance. I wasn't about to tangle with venom-mouthed animals that didn't understand I was trying to help them.

Sliding out of the bed was difficult. Hudson didn't seem to want to let me go until I pulled his finger apart myself. Poor guy. I kissed his cheek and headed off to check on Tommy. The kid was still fast asleep, his blankets over his head. I noted that he didn't have a crib at the cabin, it was more of a cave. There was a heap of blankets, a thick mattress on the ground, and a curtain hanging over the whole thing. The windows were covered in the room, the sliders nailed shut. I didn't blame them one bit. He had a talent for escaping, obviously, and a tumble down the second-story roof wouldn't have been pretty.

It wasn't until I was halfway downstairs that I smelled the trappings of breakfast: pancakes, bacon, and eggs. Someone had brought real syrup, the kind that you get when you tap a tree, not a corn stalk. I hurried down the rest of those stairs and ran into the kitchen to find Gabe and Xavion in yesterday's clothes, completely safe and sound.

I flung myself into Xavion's arms, deftly aware of the hot, greasy skillet Gabe had his hands on. Xavion picked me up and gave me a gentle twirl around the kitchen. "Missed you, too. Stopped in to check on your little animal shelter, you know. You wanna see?"

That caught my attention. He put me down and pulled out his phone as Gabe turned and kissed me. I kissed right back, only to break away as Xavion flipped through his photo album.

There, among all the trappings and work I'd put into the rescue, was an entire army of staff. I counted at least six people playing with individual dogs, each working to make them as happy as they could. And gosh, the dogs! Bosco raced across the open acreage, his tail a blur as he chased some fluffy looking ball. Carrie Ann was fast asleep on someone else's lap, her head getting stroked as she probably dreamt of cookies and belly rubs. Lady was getting her ears scratched on the back stoop, the caretaker beaming down at her.

A tear struck my cheek, unbidden. I'd been gone for just a little while and all of my work was being done for me. Had any new animals shown up? Would they know where the medication was if they needed help? What if they mis-dosed them? I sniffled and wiped my eyes. "Do they know to call Doctor Burton if there's a problem?"

"Honey, we paid a vet to go with them. There's someone on staff right now, seeing to Elijah's cracked paws. He's the big Saint Bernard mix, isn't he?" Gabe asked.

I swallowed. Elijah had been an issue. The poor dog had the worst skin I'd ever seen. "Yeah, Saint Bernard and Cocker Spaniel."

"How in the fuck did that happen?"

Leo walked into the kitchen, human once again and stealing an egg off the plate beside Gabe. There was a stack of them a mile high and Leo popped it into his mouth in one bite. He continued, "I like Elijah. Good dog. Likes to smash me into the counter top and I'm all for it, really."

I frowned. "How do *you* know Elijah?"

"No one told you? I've been making sure they're doing everything right over there. Not that they would screw it up. They're good people and they really love what you've done with the place," Leo said. "You've just been trapped by a budget, by the looks of it. And you skimp on everything that's yours. That computer's from 1994."

"2007, thank you very much," I said, scowling. "It still works. There's no reason to replace it."

"Honey, it smells like it's catching on fire when you turn it on."

It was my turn to pick up an egg and shove it in my mouth. I followed it with several strips of bacon. I didn't want to tell him he was right. I knew my computer was on its last legs; I mean it still had a CRT monitor, but it was mine. I'd worked for it and I didn't have the cash to replace it.

"Regardless," Leo said. "We bought you a new one and got you all taken care of. Full database upload, should move a lot faster now."

My jaw dropped. "You did what?"

"Bought you a new computer," Gabe said. "Four screens, too, so you can maximize what you're doing at one time. You've got so many spreadsheets on those animals, we thought it best to make sure you had a way to utilize them."

"And we paid off that vet tab," Xavion yawned, tapping a dog's picture. "Lady, right? I like her best. She just wants to be a mop on your lap and snore. Coolest dog I've met."

"You did *what*?"

I couldn't believe what I was hearing. The idea of being off the hook to Burton's clinic, that I might not have to start begging for donations just to pay them, was paramount to being told I'd won the lottery. Sure, we got some donations, but they were never enough. People out in the sticks didn't pamper their dogs like those in the city did, and I was constantly cleaning up behind them.

Whether it was fleas or teeth that desperately needed to be cleaned, I was always in the hole after taking in an animal. It worked out, because I had a little in savings. But I tried to just make payments to the clinic rather than break myself and not know when the next cash flow was coming in.

But I couldn't look at my pack as an easy way to make money. That was... wrong. They were more than that to me and I took a breath to tell them so.

"I told them to do it."

Hudson walked into the room, all power and sexuality. My eyes locked on him and my body flushed. Gabe pulled the pan off the stovetop and slid his arms around me from behind, but it was Hudson that had my attention. Of all the alphas in my life, he was the head of them. And I really wondered why.

It wasn't as if he was stronger, more handsome, or smarter than them. It wasn't that he had more money or power than the others; indeed, they seemed to own Fontaine Feeds as a group rather than as individuals. Yet, he was their CEO. He was their pack leader. He was the guy who stopped time when he walked into a room.

And for the life of me, I couldn't figure out why.

Maybe it was just plain old charisma. Some people have it. They step on stage and that presence is there in an instant. They grab everyone's attention, demand it just by the way they walk, and people either listen or they make them do it.

I definitely wasn't that person. But I wasn't going to just fall in line like a good omega, either. "But why?"

"Because I'm not having my omega living in a place that doesn't serve her goals, with equipment that's faulty, and a credit line that's about to run out when Carrie Ann might need hip surgery in the next year."

I met his gaze for the first time in what felt like forever. My brows came together, little wrinkles appearing on my forehead. "But it's so much money."

Hudson crossed the kitchen to me and cupped my cheek. He eyed me for a moment and I had to look away from him, concentrating on the tip of his nose instead. Every instinct in me wanted to fall to the floor, present, beg him to knot me again, but that certainly wasn't appropriate when we were discussing finances. I shooed it away and swallowed. "It isn't."

"There was a time and a place when I'd have agreed with you. We weren't always wealthy. When we were in college, we lived on ramen and energy drinks stolen from the cafeteria, Sadie. We know what it's like. And none of us want you to have to suffer through that."

A murmur of assent ran through the pack surrounding me. Hudson continued. "You're ours now. It doesn't matter what happens. And we take care of our own."

"Besides, there's breakfast and it's going to get cold if you keep debating about all this," Gabe said. "Everyone chow down, pack up. Let's get a move on. It's not safe here."

My alphas got plates from the cabinets, but I paused. "It's not safe here?"

"Lillian knows about the cabin, Tommy's aunt," Xavion said in way of explanation. "It could be that she tracks us down, finds you out, and decides to get aggressive before the Meet. No reason for it, but she's not the most sensible wolf I've ever met."

"Right," I said, waiting for more.

But I didn't get it. Instead, I was offered a plate. Giving in, I filled it up and headed off to the dining room to eat with the others. Hudson settled a bowl on the floor and Tommy shifted to his werewolf pup form, the way I'd met him the time he'd bit me, and dug in.

"Is that normal? Do you always feed kids off the ground?"

"Out here, yeah," Leo said. "Not where humans might see back in the city. They catch sight of Tommy and they might think we had some kind of timber wolf in the house. They'd call animal control and if Tommy shifted in front of them, you can imagine the trouble it'd cause."

I toyed with my fork, a pile of pancake on the end of it. "But out in the woods, you don't worry about paparazzi or anything like that? Like sure, there're curtains, but this place is unmonitored a lot of the time. It wouldn't be hard to put cameras up in the rafters or something."

As one, my alphas lifted their heads to look at the ceiling. I'd landed on a threat they hadn't thought about and it was as if I could hear a silent growl fill the room. Perhaps it was just because I was bonded to Hudson, with all intentions of bonding to the others, but I felt my blood rise to a simmer, if not a boil. The idea that someone had invaded my territory, fucked around with it, violated it?

I wanted to rip them apart.

It was my first conscious connection with the feral side. No wonder werewolves were always depicted as some sort of monster in books and movies. By human standards, we absolutely were.

Had I seen a dog react like that, been aggressive toward a person like that, the vet would have probably recommended euthanasia. Since I was a giant softie, I didn't usually do it. I accumulated scars and bites on my arms and legs working with the dog instead, slowly figuring out why there was aggression present in the animal and how to fix it. Most of those dogs were adopted to wonderful homes once the dog and I figured out the problem. And most of the time, it was based on fear or misunderstanding.

This wasn't. This was a primal need to protect my space, my home, my pack. It was something that was rooted in a deeper form of tribalism than humans could know.

And I added my voice to the soft, rumbling growl that was definitely audible by the time I spoke up. I was quieter than my alphas, but I still held true to the note.

"We leave after breakfast. We'll have a tech team come out, sweep this place before we use it again. She's right. Lillian could have snuck out here and she could be recording us right now. Cameras are the size of pins these days," Leo said.

Hudson sighed. "Sadie?"

I blinked over at him and frowned. He looked as if he were about to have some sort of breakdown. What on earth could be so bad that he was that upset?

"Are we welcome to move this to your place?"

Euphoria. The idea of my alphas crowded around me, my pack, my animals, everyone in one place, safe and sound? It was like taking a hit of something you got at a rave. I had to hold back tears. I was going home. *I was going home and I was taking my pack with me.* "Please. I know no one's been at my house other than your people. My neighbor would have gone over and shot them."

"Actually, your neighbor did come over and try to shoot the employees," Gabe said, helpfully. "But we talked him out of it after a few hours and a big pay-off, assuring him that the employees were there under our hire and you were being sponsored. Isn't that right, Leo?"

Leo chuckled. "I had to get the sheriff out to verify who I was. It was a blast."

"While we're there, we can make some improvements. Really see what we can do to help you. I know the roof leaks in a few places. No problem. We'll see to that." Hudson finished his plate and stood, giving me no time to object. "I'll start loading. You all finish up. Keep your eyes peeled for cameras and Sadie, keep your head down. We don't need her to find out who you are."

I shook my head. "It doesn't really matter if she does. It's not like she can go to my employer or come after me if I'm with all of you. Right?"

"Theoretically, but it's better that she never knows who you are. We don't want you bothered after the Meet, if the judges find the case in our favor."

"What if they don't?"

My alphas froze. I looked around at them and shrugged. "What if the judges don't find in my favor? I know there's some chance that they might kill me but... if they don't, then what?"

"Then we leave the area before they can hurt you. Before anyone can hurt you," Xavion said, his rage barely restrained in his voice.

Gabe shrugged. "Or we take them on as a pack, put you somewhere safe, and do what we can to give you a head start. There are other places, other supernatural communities, where they would accept a human who didn't know what she was getting herself into. But I think you'll be fine, Sadie. You're adjusting incredibly well. You'll learn more before the Meet. They don't have any reason to get rid of you. It's not like you're calling best friends or parents and telling them that you're a werewolf now, or posting selfies in wolf form. You're rational. They'll appreciate that."

I finished my breakfast and rubbed the back of my neck. "I don't want any of you hurt trying to protect me. And, obviously, I don't want to die, either. Or have Tommy get hurt. He didn't know what was going on."

"If it comes down to it," Hudson interrupted. "We'll make a decision that suits all of us. We'll remain safe, together, as a pack. And we'll do it in the smartest manner we can find. The supernatural world doesn't mix with the human world. If we must, we'll go to ground with the humans and stay away from the wild until we can move Fontaine Feeds elsewhere, outside of the reach of the locals."

It was probably the best plan we were going to have before the Meet actually happened. I didn't like the idea of putting any of them at risk, but what was I supposed to do? Instead of complaining, instead of running off into the night to save my pack the trouble of my existence, I kissed each one of them as I made my way around the table collecting plates, and headed back into the kitchen to tidy up. The dishes needed to be clean before we left, after all.

Chapter 12
Xavion

"Come on, old girl. You gonna help me put the roof on?"

I crooned to Carrie Ann, the oldest Great Dane I'd ever met, and helped her stand. She staggered for a moment, then wrapped her too-long tongue around my arm and dawdled after me. Leo had ordered supplements to help her with her joint pain and an enormous bed that Tommy had taken to sleeping on. Still, the impressive madame of Sadie's rescue would need surgery at some point to help her.

And the idea of someone putting a geriatric giant breed under anesthesia was terrifying enough that I wanted to offer her all the good times she had left.

We walked out into the snow after I put her fluffy Sherpa-style jacket on her and I'd tied on her booties. She yawned and wandered off into the field of white to pop a squat as I carried a new hammer out to Hudson, him having disappeared the last one in the snow.

Over the past week, we'd fixed kennels and built new ones. Shelters that were comfortable were now luxurious and heated even for the dogs that preferred the snow. We wanted to give them the chance to have a warm place to crash when they were done freezing themselves half to death.

After all, we understood the whole thing pretty well. As wolves, we spent our time flopping around in the drifts and barking at cars that went by, always careful to do it when we could follow the headlights and make sure they couldn't actually see us. The cold was our ideal season and the outdoor huskies of the rescue were no different.

My packmates were on the roof, Sadie inside where it was safe. They'd peeled back old, rotten shingles and replaced the tar paper underneath it. Now came the hard part; getting the new shingles to line up with the old ones. Though the whole thing needed to be torn off and repaired, that would have to wait until the snows melted. You didn't do roofing in winter unless you absolutely had to. The tar was a nightmare to work with.

"Fellas," I said, climbing the ladder and sitting down on the edge of the roof. I shimmied up to them and offered the hammer out to Hudson.

He took it with a nod of thanks. "Another hour or two and we're finished for the day. We'll head in, crash, see what Sadie's cooking."

"She's been on a roll ever since we got here. Pretty sure I smelled beef stew in the crockpot," I told him. Then I yawned. "You ever miss this life, guys? Where things are just simple and it's all quiet, no offices and just... this?"

Gabe rolled his eyes. "I don't miss having to worry about whether or not I was going to be late on the rent, or listening to someone tear my ass apart because I was five minutes late."

"And I don't miss eating the 3-week old 75% off pre-frozen hamburger from the bargain bin. That stuff always made you sick, even if you threw taco flavoring all over it," Leo said.

I shrugged and looked out across the horizon. The afternoon was getting long in the tooth and the night was coming to kill it. I let one leg dangle as Carrie Ann came over to look up at us, sitting in the snow and tilting her head. She held a frozen, mauled teddy bear in her mouth and dropped it by the ladder, an obvious demand for attention.

Well, I wasn't one to let down a lady. "I'll see you guys when you come down. I've been summoned by Her Majesty."

"Give her a good rub down for me," Hudson said. "She's a sweet girl."

I heard a thud as I climbed back down the ladder and listened to him curse. When we'd spent a month doing construction to make ends meet, the summer before we'd opened Fontaine Feeds, we'd all been black and blue. We were terrible at anything they handed us; drywall, hammering nails, driving screws- it didn't matter. We bent more damn nails and lost more tools than anyone else on the entire site.

They'd fired us within four weeks, telling us to find new careers because we damned sure weren't going to make it putting up buildings.

So, we'd gone and applied for work as slaughterhouse workers. But when we'd seen what was happening behind closed doors, Gabe had almost turned vegetarian on us. Fontaine Feeds took a while to bring together and sure, slaughterhouses were never going to be a pleasant thing. But we wanted to make sure that they were as good as they could be.

And that had brought us to where we were, putting a roof on a gorgeous omega's house and doing everything we could to secure her long-term safety.

I picked up the bear, wiggled it in the air, and Carrie Ann tried to jump to grab it. Instead, her legs went out from under her and she flopped down on her butt. Undaunted, she opened her jaws in a big, doggie laugh and struggled to her feet again. The cold, Sadie had told us, was worse on her than anything else. But I saw the weakened muscles in her hind end and knew that the hip surgery would only help the old girl so much.

But hey, we knew plenty of dog wheelchair builders. Carrie Ann would have the best that money could buy, and maybe we'd donate a few dozen to some charity while we were at it. The money never slowed down. The pet business was booming. And, if the investors were right, it was about to go through another tremendous jump. Even if we had to relocate so we could keep Sadie and Tommy safe, we'd start Fontaine Feeds back up again in no time.

And we'd be richer than ever.

The bear flew across the yard and Carrie Ann scampered off after it. She snatched it from the snow, shook it savagely, and trotted back to me with hope in her eyes. I grabbed it again and pitched it for her, sitting down on the frozen stoop as she ran off to retrieve the toy like the good girl she was.

Lady snuck out of the dog door and sat down beside me, her head resting on my arm as I waited for Carrie Ann to stop digging through the snow, stuck on entombing that poor bear again. I looked down at the little dog and tilted my head. "Does Sadie need me, miss?"

She looked up at me, blinking large, sad eyes. Obviously, she had no idea what I meant or even what I'd asked. All she knew was that I'd said Sadie's name. It was likely that she couldn't find her, leading her to hunt down one of us instead. I assumed that Sadie was upstairs dealing with the birds; she'd said she'd be taking them their afternoon snack.

That meant Sadie was behind the baby gates, up a long staircase that Lady probably wasn't comfortable with. Carrie Ann happily meandered past me as I picked up Lady and opened the door, taking them both back inside. One of the three huskies that lived outside, largely due to the destruction that happened when they were inside, howled as the door shut behind me.

Instinct took over. I tipped my head back and howled right along with the dog. My pack mates took up the call on the roof and I heard both Sadie and Tommy from upstairs, howling with the rest of us.

The dog shut up pretty quickly. Most pet dogs aren't particularly fond of wolves. I cuddled Lady as I walked upstairs, making sure to close the gate at the bottom after me. Sadie had been gone for just a short time, but Carrie Ann had been in better shape when she'd left. The Great

Dane didn't need to lose her footing on the stairs and crash land at the bottom.

On the landing, I plopped Lady on the ground and walked along the hallway. I peeked into the bird room to find Sadie kneeling on the ground as Tommy, awestruck by the giant cockatoo on Sadie's arm, stroked the bird's chest. It preened itself, never so much as raising a claw at our boy. "Smart bird."

Sadie looked over at me and smiled. "She was abandoned by her people about six years ago. She kept saying rude words to the neighbors and no one wanted to deal with that. Took me a couple of days to get her to stop."

"I don't know how you keep up with all their stories like that," I said, coming to stroke the bird as well.

Her eyes pinned, the pupil narrowing, and she stared at me. I cocked my head at the cockatoo. "What? You like the puppy but not the mutt?"

She fluffed her... is it a crest? I don't know what it's called, but they have that floofy feather head thing that happens. Then they usually rock out, if it's a viral video. Either way, she looked pissed so I took my hand away from her before I got bit.

Get your paw caught in an old bear trap? It sucks.

Get bit by a bird? Fuck that.

"Lady here wanted to see what was going on upstairs, so I thought I'd bring her up to say hi," I told Sadie.

Tommy was immediately distracted from the bird, his attention focused on the scrappy little dog that toddled up to him. He screamed and grabbed her, wrapping his arms around her neck and squeezing like he was about to pull her head off. For her part, Lady just licked his face and dealt with it. I gently pried him off of her and eyed him, a growl not quite making its way from the back of my throat.

The kid knew better. He hunkered at me, then leaned forward to touch the tip of his human nose to the little dog's.

"Better," I said, just as my phone vibrated in my pocket. I frowned at it, picked it up, and raised a brow at the unregistered number. "One second, Sadie."

Without waiting for an answer, I turned and left the room. I walked across to the bathroom, shut the door, and answered. "Hello?"

"You wolves never answer your phones," sighed a dark, smoky voice filled with disappointment.

I returned the sigh. "Eskal. Why are you calling me before the Meet? The rest of your flight finds out and you're toast."

"I never worry myself with the emotions of those beneath me," the dragon sneered. "Lillian is pushing for a dark moon Meet. We told her no. I rather thought you would be pleased with the opportunity of another week and a half of existence before the unicorns wipe your worthless pelts from the world."

I struggled to maintain my calm. While we'd never had personal problems with the dragon flight that lived in the neighboring town, we'd never exactly been friendly, either. Wolves and dragons weren't legendary enemies, but there was enough drama between the various packs and the numerous flights that we kept our distance from one another to be somewhat polite.

But it was a cool politeness, the sort you have with rude co-workers who borrow your stapler and never give it back.

"Are you threatening my pack?" I asked, finally, mastering my want to go see if dragon ribs tasted the same as that lizard I crunched once.

Eskal purred into the phone. "It's more like a promise. You illegally turned a human into one of yours. That's a threat to our flight and the security of the rest of the supernatural community. Unless she's an impressive creature, smart and clever enough to get all of you out of trouble, I'll be glad to roast you. Personally."

The phone hung up, as if he were punctuating the remark. I rolled my eyes at it and shoved it away, but I had to admit that it rattled me a little. We'd all seen the occasional problem member get fricasseed. I didn't want to see Lillian's satisfied gaze as we were led to the platform and-

...No. No, she'd save Tommy. She'd take him under her wing and demand clemency for the kid. He was just a puppy, he couldn't have known what was happening or what he was doing. She'd blame Hudson and the rest of us, making it some kind of sexual thing. And, sure, we enjoyed our time with Sadie. Mating was a natural, wonderful thing to partake in. And being with her felt more like love than anything I'd ever experienced before.

Sadie understood us. She *got* us, as individuals and as a pack. More than that, she cared about what happened to us. How many omegas would have just turned themselves over to the judgment of the supernatural community, hunkered, and begged not to be killed? Instead, Sadie was dedicating as much time as she could to learning about the culture and what would be expected of her.

In the past week, she'd already come to shift under her own willpower. She knew what not to say, how to react to fear that begged her to shapeshift, and ways to manage the scent she left everywhere she went. We had to deal with some dogs not liking us, but there were ways to mask that scent. Considering that she was so passionately involved in rescue, it was a necessity that she mastered it.

But she had. She'd done it in a day, passing by strange dogs without so much as them turning their head to look at her. We were giving her our A-game, and she was, too.

I slipped out of the bathroom and headed back downstairs. Carrie Ann was fast asleep with the other Dane, Matilda, both of them flopped on a mattress the size of a queen bed. I went to Her Majesty, removed her boots and jacket, and hung them up by the door as I left to speak with Hudson.

...Who was still busy hammering his hands. I climbed the ladder, walked up the icy roof, and turned on my phone. Then I scrolled to the unregistered number and showed it to the rest of the alphas. "Eskal called. Said he wants us all dead. Real friendly conversation, the son of a bitch."

"Think he's in Lillian's pocket?" Leo asked.

Hudson put the hammer down and shook his head. "Doesn't matter. If he is, we're fucked. If he isn't, one of the judges might be. She keeps calling all of us. I think she wants to brag."

"If we run now, we never have to face them," I said, but I knew I was dreaming. None of us were cowards. We weren't going anywhere.

The hammer began to slip. I caught it with my toe and sat down with the others. Hudson took my phone and scowled at it. "We need a better plan."

"We can't plan if we don't know what we're up against," Gabe said. "If you'd just talk to Lillian, she'd probably screw up and say something to you. She's too stupid to brag without giving the game away."

"What game?"

I jerked and looked over at Sadie, who'd climbed the ladder as we talked. Silent, our sneaky little omega crept onto the roof and came to sit on Leo's lap. He wrapped an arm protectively around her stomach but I could see the worry in his face. The roof was pretty high up and we'd told her not to come up unless she had to. Better if we got hurt trying to help her than if she fell and busted something.

Gabe shook his head. "Lillian keeps calling. And a dragon just called to be a creep to Xav. It doesn't really change anything, but the odds may be tipping further against us."

"Lillian keeps calling?" Sadie asked.

Hudson eyed her. "It's not important. If we just ignore her, she'll stop calling eventually. And there's no reason to worry about it. She's controlled where she is, and she can't possibly get to us. She doesn't know you exist."

"I know that. And while I appreciate that, maybe her mind would change if I talked to her."

"No!" I said, three other voices joining mine.

Sadie looked around at us, then rolled her eyes. "I've dealt with worse. Come on. Give me your phone, Hudson. I won't tell her anything important. I just want to know who I'm up against. Maybe I can come up with something to outwit her."

He hesitated. I sighed and offered mine over. "She's in the contacts. Don't stay on longer than a few minutes. I don't know if tracing works on these phones, but if it does, she's likely to have someone trying to do it."

She nodded, took the phone, and kissed Leo's forehead as she slid away. I watched as she descended the ladder once more and held my breath until she was on the ground. She went back into the house and I looked back at my alpha pack mates, trying to keep the worry out from under my skin.

It didn't work. Hudson grabbed a hammer and beat the shit out of a nail, bending it and breaking it as the rest of us ground our teeth. Lillian didn't need to be within breathing room of Sadie, much less on a phone call with her. But it wasn't like we had any choice. We weren't about to deny our omega what she wanted, and if she wanted to talk to Lillian? Well, that's what she was going to do.

I tried to focus on something else, but it just wouldn't come. We'd found happiness only for it to fall to pieces before our eyes. The Meet was coming sooner than any of us wanted.

And no matter what we did, no matter how well Sadie performed, I had a feeling that we were fucked.

Chapter 13
Sadie

My thumb hovered over the call button. I only knew the woman by reputation, but steeling myself for the upcoming conversation was the least I could do. The phone cupped in one hand, I ran the opposite over Bosco's giant head and considered my options.

I guessed that I could simply not call her. I could go into the Meet as blind as the rest of my pack was, only assuming why she had such an enormous bone to pick with me. That wasn't what I wanted to do, so I knocked that off the list.

I could head into town in the night, find her place; there was an address attached to the contact on Xav's phone, and try to speak with her in person. I'd get her body language down, perhaps see more than I would simply by speaking with her. I'd watch her movements and attempt to understand if she was lying to me, if she was playing me into a trap.

Though I had to admit, I'd never been very good at things like that. Heck, I'd almost ended up playing a Carrie role at my senior prom for no other reason than I thought I'd finally made pals with the popular kids. I'd been blindsided when they tried to take pictures of me making out with a guy behind the gym, like so many other class members were doing at the same time. Yet they hadn't mattered; only I had.

I really hated to be a target.

"Please enjoy this playback music while your party is reached," chirped the phone.

Beethoven's 5th blared out of the speaker, horrible and tinny. It sounded as if they were playing it on a rusty washboard. I waited for ten, fifteen seconds, then pulled the phone away from my ear and reached for the end call slider.

"Xavion?"

Her voice was gentle, a quality I hadn't really imagined her having. I frowned at the phone as my finger hovered, debated myself once again, and gave in. "Not exactly. My name's Sadie and you're the one threatening my pack. ...Because of me?"

"Sadie!" She gasped, her tone thicker than honey during a blizzard. "Oh, goodness gracious. I didn't expect to get a call from you. How are you? Are you adjusting well?"

I hadn't expected that, either, but I was a newbie to the world of werewolf warfare. Maybe you were fake-nice to people for a time before you ripped their guts out? I cleared my throat. "I think things are coming along well. Tommy's the sweetest kid I've ever met and the guys seem to like me well enough. But I don't think that's the focus of the conversation, ma'am."

"Oh honey, don't ma'am me. We're just a pair of bitches having a quick conversation, aren't we?"

Were female werewolves really called that? I added it to the internal, ever-growing list of things to ask one of my pack mates. At this point, I was going to run out of time asking them questions. "I guess we are."

"Of course. I just want to be sure those boys aren't brutalizing you. They're a rough pack to get bonded to. I know. My sister was part of it and they went and got her killed," she paused, tears in her voice. I could almost see her dabbing at either eye with a handkerchief. "Terrible thing that it was, I want my nephew to be safe. I'm sure you understand. And Hudson lets him loose in the woods in freaking winter, lets him ruin your life-"

"My life isn't anywhere near ruined," I broke in. "And I adore Tommy. He really seems to like me, too."

"Well yes, darling, but any little alpha would be taken up with an omega. But I know you don't understand what I'm saying, I'm sorry. I'll try not to speak too far above your head."

I felt as though I'd been slapped. I drew the phone back and put it on speaker mode, just so I wouldn't have to have her voice closer to my ear. Maybe all werewolf women, I really hated the term bitches, were like this. Though it wasn't as if I were swimming in friends before, with few people understanding my need to care for the animals of my county, it would have been nice to have the potential of being around a few women like me.

Maybe it was best to try to make friends with her. I'd have been displeasured with the sort of woman who came in and replaced my sister, if I'd had any, too. "I'm trying to understand all of it. The guys- sorry, my pack, thinks that I'm doing a good job of it."

"They would. You know I called the Meet to protect Tommy and you, right? You know that?"

I took a breath and a flood of disgust came out of me. "I think that you called the Meet because you're still mad at Hudson for getting your sister killed. I think that you called the Meet because you want to see him and my other alphas suffer as much as you can and this is the perfect opportunity for it. And I think that maybe your sister is better off dead than having to deal with you."

Well, so fucking much for making friends with her. Where had all of that come from? A warm, cozy sensation uncoiled within me, as if I'd just settled down for a family movie with my entire pack. Whatever I'd done, the others somehow knew about it. And they were pleased with me.

How they felt meant a hell of a lot more than making friends with her.

"You just don't understand," she sighed, miserable. "Let me make it up to you. One quick little visit. We sit down, we talk, and I see if they're really doing right by you, by all of us in the community. The law is the law, Sadie, no matter how sweet you are. And Hudson should have had my nephew under his control. If I find you safe and sound, for yourself and for the matters of the Supernatural Secrecy Pact, I'll drop the Meet."

I paused and looked at Bosco. The dog was fast asleep, my hand still resting on his big, empty head. I chewed my lower lip and thought about it. It could be a trap. Oh, by all means, it probably was a trap. But what was she going to do to me? Kill me in the middle of some restaurant? That didn't seem likely. And she sure wasn't going to invite me to her house. She didn't trust me. You didn't invite people to your home when you didn't trust them.

"We meet somewhere public, somewhere without the guys?"

"Somewhere right out in the wide open where everyone would see me, or you, become a wolf. We'd be in violation of the Pact immediately and that would be that. Can't exactly call a Meet if I'm being a bad girl, now can I?"

I didn't see any way she could hurt me. But how was I going to sneak away from my alphas? They had all but barred me from leaving, not quite saying that they didn't want me to go or taking my keys, but always giving me worried looks and asking if I wanted them to join me. I guess I expected that. I hadn't wanted them to leave either, when they'd had to; mostly to go get more wood or screws or whatever they needed to keep improving the rescue.

There were some people who would have taken offense to them penning me in, but I knew what their hearts were. I knew that they were just scared, like I was, that someone might hurt me. Or maybe that my car would stall on train tracks. Life came at you fast when you loved other people, even if they could turn into wolves.

"You're buying," I told her.

She laughed in response and I sighed. "Where are we meeting up? And when? It's going to be a trick and a half to get them off my tail."

"Just throw a little bleach in the road. It won't hurt them and they won't be able to track you, sweetie. Is Alfonzo's too much of a drive for you? Around 6 tomorrow?"

God, she'd named one of the most expensive Italian restaurants in the tri-state area. Well, if she was going to wine and dine me, it was hard to say no. I'd had the worst craving in the world for garlic bread and I had no idea if I could eat it. Dogs couldn't have garlic. Could werewolves?

"I'll be there," I said, and hung up on her without giving her the chance to say goodbye. It gave me a flicker of satisfaction.

Bleach the road to get away from the guys, leave them at the rescue with a note of apology, go meet the evil queen in a castle made of spaghetti. God, life had gotten weird since I'd been bitten.

It felt so wrong. I was, without a doubt, absolutely betraying their trust. They hadn't even wanted me to talk to her and I was planning to sneak away on them. I sighed, shook my head, and headed back outside to return Xav's phone. My alphas were just putting everything away as I came up on them. "Xav? Your phone?"

He took it and drew me close, worry written all over his face. "What'd she do to you? You smell like you've been through a nightmare."

"She's not that bad," I said, and made a decision on the fly. "I'm meeting up with her tomorrow at 6. I'll make sure you guys have something to eat before I go, unless you want me to bring you something back?"

His grip on me tightened. "The hell you are."

As the others moved to surround me, I yanked out of his grasp and stepped back, facing the group of them. I pulled myself up to my full height and lifted my chin, the picture of all kinds of stubborn. "I'm going. She told me to bleach the ground when I left so none of you could follow me. That's not fair to you, so I'm not doing it. But I'm going, and you don't have any right to stop me."

"We don't have any right, and we're not going to force you to stay with us," Hudson said. "But we have every right to be concerned about you. We're pushing too hard? Fine. Tell us. You just did. It's not safe. She's not safe. She hasn't been right since Becca died."

"Lillian always sucked, but that broke her," Gabe frowned.

Leo reached out to me. I took his hand and he drew me into his arms. The others followed him, a big huddle of puppies. "We're just worried about you. We already suffered one loss, Sadie. Can you blame us for being jumpy?"

"I could blame you, but it wouldn't be right," I said, leaning into his chest. Then I smiled up at him. "I could take all your minds off of it, for a little while."

Gabe and Hudson gave quiet growls. The pack of alphas around me tightened in formation and I squirmed out from them. "Catch me if you can."

And off I ran, straight into the house. They'd been there for a week or so, I'd lived there a huge portion of my life. I knew every nook, every cranny, and I was going to use them to my advantage. I took off for the nearly hidden linen closet upstairs and heard feet pounding behind me. I ducked away, dove through a bedroom door, and listened to those feet trot off in another direction.

For now, at least, they were using their eyes not their noses. When they did, I'd be in trouble. And to be perfectly honest, I was surprised that my distraction had worked. My men were wonderfully smart.

Too smart for such a ploy. Xavion caught me around the waist as I burst out of the bedroom, intent on the linen closet. He cheered out to the others, "I got her!"

I laughed and demanded he let me go, squirming in his grasp. Delight and the promise of carnal pleasure pulsed through me, my connection with the rest of the pack burning with lust. He carried me into my bedroom and I grabbed him by the hair, kissing him as he bore me into the mattress.

Gabe showed up first, our first-time duo completed once more. He chucked his shirt across the way, stripping himself as he came toward us. Xav growled at him, pulled him close, and pressed him into me as well.

Leo was next, his eyes snapping with feral intent. He prowled to the bed, climbed on it, and I reached for his top. My hand caught it, grabbed the front, and tore the buttons off. They scattered across the mattress, me, and the floor, and I pulled him down with the rest of us.

It wasn't until Hudson joined that the fervor of the room changed. He came to me as I waited, sitting up in the bed and staring at him. Slowly, he left his shoes by the door and watched as the boys surrounded me. The three of them were on their hands and knees, their fingers spread upon the surface of the bed as if they intended to keep him from joining us by taking up as much space as they could.

His eyes narrowed and he strode across the room, a king among kings, and looked down at me. Like the first picture I'd seen of him, it took my breath away. I met him, eye to eye, and he descended on me. His teeth snapped into the mark on my neck, breaking and refreshing it. Hands tore at my clothes, shucking them from me in a thrilling, breathless instant. I arched off the bed as someone's teeth bit into a nipple, a cry of agonized ecstasy bursting from my throat.

On my little twin bed, in the room I'd grown up in, I'd dreamt of terrifying monsters; feral animals, who would tear me apart. And in that perfect moment, they did. Hudson shattered me in twain, Gabe brought me back together, and Xavion and Leo took turns ruining and fixing me time and time again.

I lost track of who was where, knowing only that someone was between my legs hilted deep in that sweet spot. A second alpha was busy marking me as his own, taking what Hudson had already claimed on the opposite side of my neck. A third offered himself to me and I took that beautiful, uncut, dark cock into my mouth. The fourth was fixated on my pleasure, demanding that I writhe and buck in time with the others.

And I did. My body was no longer my own, falling to pieces under the needs of my men and loving every moment of it.

Over and over again I was filled, filled to bursting. Each of my alphas took their turn, and I took their knot. While we were tied, the three that remained loose kept me occupied. Kisses were exchanged, hands explored, and I was completely enraptured by their flesh as they were mine.

When, at last, Leo lay over my back completely exhausted, his knot buried deep within me, the pack collapsed as one. We fell to the mattress, which was far too small for all the hijinks we had just kicked up, and panted for all we were worth. Every inch of me tingled, every part exhausted.

"There's beef stew downstairs," I whispered.

And my alphas, breathless and entirely satisfied, laughed.

I felt them, all of them at once, as if I were physically attached to them. We were a pack, truly one pack, and the difference between simply being bonded to Hudson and being bonded to all of them at once, was astounding. I crawled into Xavion's arms, Leo kissing the big man as we piled up on my bed and fell into a restful state; that glorious twilight between actual sleep and merely resting.

We only parted after Leo's knot had shrunk enough to slide away from me. I didn't want the shower that waited for me. I wanted to smell like my alphas, a mixture of fragrances that intoxicated me, for as long as I could. But the human side of my mind was hardwired to accept nothing else. I showered, mourning the loss of their scent, and went downstairs while they did the same.

Hudson brought Tommy down with him, the others following bit by bit. I pulled warm, fresh bread bowls from the oven and loaded them down with the stew. We settled around the dinner table shortly thereafter, the dogs joining us. Bosco rested his head on my thigh and I slipped bits of beef to him, as was our typical nightly ritual.

Outside, snowflakes drifted past the window lazily. Our little home lit up the night, pushing away the impending darkness and releasing warmth into a frigid, uncaring world.

I looked around at the table as my alphas chatted, not quite part of the conversation but rather listening in on it. Xavion and Gabe were debating about what project they wanted to do the next day, but if the snow kept up, I'd end up snuggling down in their arms instead; at least until I had to leave for my meeting.

I glanced up at the ceiling and watched for a moment. My alphas' roof work was the fix I had needed. No drip of snow, no drop of water permeated the night sky mural painted above my head. And there, mingled with every star in the universe, was Her.

The moon, only a painting but still, gazed lovingly down at us and cemented something in that moment.

This was where I belonged, where I had always belonged.

And no bitch was going to take that from me.

Chapter 14
Sadie

We awoke the next morning to a problem.

If I were going to head into town, the roads had to be shoveled enough to let me do it. My tiny sedan wasn't going to make it over the drifts and I'd end up in the trees if I tried to run over three feet of the white stuff.

No matter how much my men dug, cursed, and threw their backs into it, it just kept coming down. Tommy and I watched from the porch, him as a puppy all wrapped up in every small dog winter accessory I owned, and me in three separate coats while I clung to my hot cocoa.

Though I had to admit, it wasn't so much that I was cold. I just loved the trappings of the season; the steamy mug in my hands, the cozy clothing wrapped around my body, the penchant for snuggling in with your loved ones in front of a roaring fire. I couldn't wait until I soothed Lillian's feelings that evening and got the whole Meet taken care of behind closed doors. Maybe we could take the dogs with us out to the cabin, really get that fireplace going, and teach Tommy about roasting marshmallows.

I nuzzled into the puppy who had given me a new lease on life. "I owe you the world, kid. And I don't take that lightly. I hope you know that."

In answer, he wiggled from my grasp and ran off to the corner of the yard to chase his tail. Gosh, didn't I know that feeling? The simple fact that it was likely I'd never have to worry about not having enough cash on hand to take care of an ailing dog was incredible.

...But the possibility that we might have to leave the area to save our lives? How would I help the local animals if that happened?

I had to ace this meetup with Lillian. I just.. I *had* to.

Around four in the afternoon, the guys gave in. There was too much snow and not enough hands on deck to dig through it. What we really needed was-

"Listen to me," Hudson said, picking me up from the stoop. I'd half frozen myself to it throughout the day. He plopped a set of keys in my hands. I'd have recognized that giant H logo anywhere. "Take the Hummer. I know it's a big, stupid car and... kind of douchey, when you get down to it. But it does what it needs to do and it can handle a piddly little snowstorm like this."

I fastened my hand around the keys. It was practically permission, maybe even encouragement, to go try to work this out on my own. "'Piddly little', huh? You're starting to sound like you belong out here in the sticks."

"I grew up in the middle of nowhere, Sadie. And I still prefer it." He leaned down and kissed me, his lips cold against mine. Then he did something I hadn't expected. He hugged me tight and sighed against my ear. "If anything happens to you, I don't know what I'll do."

Every ounce of bravado I had sank to the cold, dark depths inside of me. I pressed my head beneath his chin and tightened my gloved hands on his coat. "I'll be okay. We'll all be okay after this. She said she'd drop the Meet if I'm impressive, and you guys sure seem to think I'm something great."

"You *are*," he growled, scenting me.

His 5-o'clock shadow brushed over my forehead and I clenched the keys. The temptation to beg him and the others to accompany me was out of this world, but some part of me knew Lillian wouldn't like that.

Would I? I'd see it as being ganged up on, a threat and a display of one. It would be all she needed to point out that I wasn't tough enough for her world, that I was just some weak-willed person getting dragged around by Hudson and the others.

I couldn't let that in her mind, even for a minute. I drew away from Hudson, kissed the bobble of his Adam's apple, and went to seek out the others. Gabe was asleep, exhausted from digging. I kissed his forehead. Xavion? I found him taking a shower, but I wrote him a quick note and slid it beneath the door.

Leo brooded over a sandwich in the kitchen. "I understand why you're going. But I wish you wouldn't."

"I wish I didn't have to go, either," I said. "But Hudson gave me the Hummer's keys. At least I'll have that. And it's got some kind of tracking software on it, right? So, if she gets really nuts, you can always just hunt me down that way."

His shoulders relaxed. "It still isn't safe."

"Nothing is."

He sighed and abandoned the sandwich, wrapping an arm around my waist and drawing me into his lap. "Nothing is, but there's a difference between getting rear-ended and running across an interstate tempting fate."

"I'm not-" I tried to argue, but he kissed me. I melted against him, helpless to resist.

When he broke away, he rested his forehead against mine. "We love you, Sadie Faye. Stay safe."

"I love you guys, too," I whispered. "I'll try."

The promise felt so final. Leo let me go, picked up the sandwich, and went back to staring at it. My poor alphas. All they wanted to do was protect me, but I was so busy running into the fire to protect them that they were at a loss.

I couldn't imagine that it was a common thing. Omegas seemed to be there to clean house, take care of the kids, and enjoy a comfortable life with a guardian that cherished them. Alphas got fulfillment out of it, and I was absolutely ruining any chance they had of finding that.

But I hadn't been the one who had called the Meet.

One of the guys had poured salt along the walk to keep it from icing up. I still half-skated down it to the Hummer. With a last, longing look at the house, I composed myself and got in the beast of a vehicle. It started up on the first turn of the key and I stared at it in wonder. My car would've taken four or five times to get going.

"You better get used to it, Sadie," I told myself. "Because your boys are never gonna let you deal with that kind of stuff again."

The drive was a quiet one, taking way too much time and too much effort. I only slid off the road a few times, each one easily corrected. Though I had to admit, I doubted the restaurant would be open. Who went out in messes like the one I was dealing with, if they had a choice?

Yet the restaurant was open, and it was packed. There was a line out the door, deep into the snow, and I had to park two blocks away to find a place that fit the Hummer. I slid the keys into my coat pocket and hurried back toward the front door.

I knew Lillian the moment I saw her. It was in the way she stood, the way she moved, the way she processed what she saw. I realized the subtle difference between what our kind must look like against the humans that moved around us. We were still, quiet, predatory. Our looks were just a little too sharp, our springs a little too tightly wound.

I hadn't expected her to be a nun. The habit was a polite, flowing thing that fit every stereotype most people have about nuns. Still, I thought the black and white was nice if not exactly practical in the snow. She looked a bit like a penguin.

"Lillian?" I asked, clutching my purse with one hand.

She turned to me and smiled, her teeth coming to points. "Sadie, sweetheart. You should have used the valet parking. I'd have paid for it for you."

I held my breath for a moment, got control of myself, and tried not to let her see my knees knocking. She put me off balance. Was she an alpha? An omega? I didn't know. My senses weren't that good, yet. But she had something about her that bothered me deeply, something that just didn't feel right.

Maybe it was just because I didn't like being away from my pack.

"I appreciate the offer, but Hudson and the others really don't mind taking care of what I need. The back of the line's about thirty people thattaways," I said, nodding away from the front door.

Lillian blinked at me, then tossed her head back in a laugh. "Oh, you sweet thing. We don't wait."

And she marched right up to the podium and demanded her reservation. When the server tried to explain that we were twenty minutes late, she cocked her head to the side and I was certain she was about to rip his throat out. The guy gave in, grabbed a couple of menus, and swept us off to our table before Lillian had to get violent.

I followed, silent and trying to gather my thoughts. I hadn't expected this sort of treatment or the fact that she had the power to give it. I'd expected her to be a curt, tough older woman who wanted to tear my head off my shoulders.

We were seated at a window where we could watch the people shivering outside. A few weeks ago, I wouldn't have considered dining here, much less being seated like that. At best, I'd have been one of the poor souls out in the snow.

"Most of the staff here know me," Lillian said. "And you don't worry about the check, they'll put it on my account."

I shook my head. "You're the oddest nun I've ever met in my life."

"I can't imagine you meet very many of us. We're a dying breed. Much like another little issue of yours. Tell me, how does Tommy deal with you?"

The server brought a bottle of wine, showed us the label, and I realized I had no idea what I was looking for on it; that I was merely trying to get my bearings. Every time she spoke, it was to throw me off balance. She practically had me doing cartwheels just trying to keep up with her. Why would she start with Tommy? "He likes me well enough. He's the reason I'm here. I think Hudson probably told you he wasn't, but he's just trying to take care of his kid."

She listened to me, taking a sip of the wine and watching me over the glass. She cursed, she drank, and she acted like a princess. It wasn't like I'd gone to catholic school or anything, but Lillian just got weirder the longer I was near her. Over the course of the next hour, I was certain I never wanted to see her again. She loathed my men and acted as if Tommy was a prize to be won, not a kid who was great because he *was*.

Another bottle of wine was delivered. I hesitated, knowing I had a long drive home ahead of me. "I don't know."

"You'll wear it off before you get anywhere near a car," she assured me. "Enjoy yourself. It's cold outside. That stuff'll warm you right up."

I watched the server pour my glass full and I fought with myself. I'd already had an entire glass, while Lillian drank down most of the other bottle. Two wouldn't put me over the limit, but the conditions outside were treacherous enough. I needed to be ready to skid to a halt if some idiotic deer jumped out in front of me.

But it was so rare that I got the good stuff, and that was all the restaurant seemed to serve. I didn't know much about wine, but the server had acted as though the second bottle was even better than the first; and the first had been incredible.

I picked up the glass and took a tiny sip. A rich, warmness seeped into my veins, inviting me to have another sip and see what happened. When I hesitated, Lillian waved me on. "Do it. You won't get a vintage like this again. Hudson's terrible about wines, he prefers those terrible fruity drinks. Who ever met an alpha who wanted to drink daiquiris?"

I couldn't resist. She was terrible, but she was right. I wanted the wine and hadn't I been through enough to deserve it? I tipped back the glass and shook my head at her. "He can have whatever he wants and you really don't have any right to criticize him."

The words came out of me, but they felt as though they were being spoken from a dozen yards away. I frowned and rubbed my throat, a chill overtaking my skin. I'd taken my coat off on the way in, but the cold hadn't really bothered me throughout the night. Now, my skin prickled and gooseflesh trotted along my arms. I shivered, the first time since I'd-

Oh.

Oh no.

My pack had been distant since I left the house, but now they were a million miles out of reach. I tried to remember their individual scents, the way they tasted when I kissed them, the quivering release of their mating, and found nothing. The memories were intact, but the complex, visceral reaction I'd gotten used to wasn't there.

"You...?" I asked, desperately wanting it to not be true.

Lillian only smiled at me, her head tilting. In a calm, measured movement, she reached out and knocked the rest of the bottle to the floor. The evidence soaked into the carpet, spilling away forever.

"Oopsie."

I ran.

Grabbing my coat from the back of the chair, I hurled myself from the restaurant. I had no way to know if she wanted to follow me, no way to know which employees were friends of Lillian's. Everyone looked the same to me, the predatory features gone to my vision. All I could smell was the pasta, marinara seeping into every frame of my being. I flew through the front doors and narrowly avoiding collision with the line of people waiting to get in.

I wanted to tell them, to warn them that there was a monster inside. That the woman who had lured me out under the guise of trying to resolve the problems between my new family and her own had poisoned me. No, her weapon hadn't been poison. It had been deceit. She'd stripped me of everything, of everyone, and I didn't know what was happening. I didn't know, I didn't know, *I didn't know*.

My heart hammered my ribs as I caught the handle on the Hummer. The door didn't open and I cried out, slapping the big, stupid hunk of metal. I clawed through my pockets, intent on the keys. The unlock button wasn't right, nothing was right, but I hit every pad on the key ring until I heard the doors click open. In I went, huddling on the driver's seat and curling my arms tight around my knees.

At last, I tipped my head back and howled into the frozen night, my instincts giving a final, mournful cry.

And then they were gone.

I pulled down the vanity mirror and yanked my scarf off to look at my neck. My pale skin was fine, whole and unharmed. I burst into tears. Where were my alphas? Where was my pack? Every mark they'd left on me, imbibing me with some part of themselves, was missing.

Hadn't my pack said there was no return to humanity after they'd given me the wrong pills? It'd been a panic, but I remembered that. It had been the moment when my entire life changed, when I'd finally stepped on the road to being a whole, happy person with lovers who adored me and I them. We'd only just begun, I'd been so excited, so fascinated by what awaited all of us.

And it was gone.

Over.

Empty.

I was a knocked-over bucket, a tipped vase, an upside-down cup. There was nothing left, but I couldn't wrap my mind around that. Surely, at any moment, I would feel my pack link back up with me. I would know what they were doing, know that they were worried about me. I would know... something, anything.

All I knew was that I'd ruined the one good thing I had. I sobbed into the steering wheel, my forehead resting over the horn. The first one took me by surprise, but by the second I gave in. The tears poured down my face and I fell to pieces, sorrow eating me alive from within.

My phone rang. I coughed, trying to compose myself, and pulled it out of my pocket. The number was unlisted. "Hello?"

"Just so you know, darling, I'm still calling the Meet. You'll just be a little extra crispy by the end of the night. Ta-ta."

Lillian hung up on me without waiting for a reply. I stared at the blank phone screen and hiccupped, my heart a cinder of what it had been before I'd been stupid enough to trust her.

I was no longer a werewolf, but I would still hang for the crimes I hadn't committed.

I was no longer a werewolf, but she was still trying to ruin the people I loved.

I was no longer a werewolf, but that fucker wasn't getting my little boy.

Fury boiled up inside me and I turned the Hummer over, murder in my heart. I shifted the vehicle into drive and barely controlled myself from peeling down the street. If I was going to ruin Lillian's plans and save my pack. No matter if I had fur or flesh, I'd have to make it home in one piece.

And when I did, when I was done crying, I was going to rip her fucking throat out.

Chapter 15
Hudson

"Think she'd like it if we took her on a hunt, if they give us approval to keep her?" Gabe asked.

I sighed and poked at my leftover lasagna with a fork, staring at my plate. "I don't know, Gabe."

There was nothing I wanted less than to sit and try to figure out what we'd do after the Meet. It was drawing closer and my nerves were shot. Another week, to the day, and we'd be facing judgment. I still hadn't managed to put together a good defense. Love meant nothing to the law.

The dragons would see me as weak, a slave to my emotions. The griffins would laugh at me, but they rarely mated for more than a season and just to raise chicks. The cats would get it, but they prided themselves on being law-abiding citizens of the supernatural community.

And the unicorns? God, if the unicorns showed up, they might be lenient. Of everyone, they were the most rational semi-immortals running around. Still, I knew it would be a challenge to convince them.

In truth, I was still having trouble convincing myself. I loved Sadie; we all did. We hadn't had her for very long, why tell us we couldn't? I mourned that which was almost certainly going to be, that which hadn't become yet. But I was certain that nothing good could come of it.

Lillian would see to it.

God, why had I let Sadie go? I jabbed a layer of noodle and meat into my mouth and tried to remember where we'd stashed the Tylenol. Medication had to be stored practically on the ceiling to keep curious, taller dogs from getting into something they shouldn't touch.

As I swallowed, searing pain ripped through my chest. It was if someone had reached into my ribcage and tore my heart out. I fell from my chair, *again*, hitting the ground hard on my shoulder, and screamed. A quadruplet of voices answered my cry and I heard Gabe slap onto the floor beside me. Something had happened; something had happened to Sadie and we were too far away to stop it.

My alpha brain panicked. There are instances when we are far from being in control of ourselves, even as rational and tightly-wound men. I bucked off the linoleum the second I could and hauled myself to my feet. Gabe beat me to the door, leaving Sadie's keys hanging on the wall. I retrieved them and followed him out, limping as if I'd been hit by a car.

It wasn't just the physical pain, there was something wrong. I felt hollow, like someone had reached into me with an ice cream scoop and simply peeled away all the goodness I'd had recently. I'd been drained, ripped apart, in seconds and that had never happened.

No, I was wrong. I'd experienced it once before, when Tommy's mother had died in the woods. I'd known when she passed, what had happened, and then it was only the work of collecting her body that had lain before us. The others had known it, felt it, but not like what I'd experienced.

If Lillian had killed Sadie, she'd be in prison by the end of the night. Even the humans weren't so relaxed about a murder in plain sight. I didn't think she'd be so cocksure as to do it, but you never knew. As Gabe screamed in frustration, I threw him the keys and pulled out my phone.

Sadie didn't answer.

I tried Lillian instead. No answer.

I called the restaurant and sighed, relieved, when the phone was picked up. The background sounded perfectly normal, a quiet evening dinner for the upper-class set. Soft music tinkled through the drone of voices, never quite so loud as a Macaroni Grill or an Olive Garden, but loud enough to reassure me. It was a stage set for casual disappointment at ridiculous prices.

Perfect for people with too much to spend and too little experience with the world.

"Excuse me," I said. "I don't suppose a Sadie Adelaine is present at your establishment tonight?"

I gave him a quick description of our lover, to which he asked me to wait. The line was left open, a sign of glaring mismanagement. Had I been attempting to run a facade of that stature, that slip alone would have cost him his job. Thankfully for him, I'd never had an interest in becoming a restauranteur.

He returned quickly enough, had my mate not been in danger. As it was, there was a distinct struggle in controlling myself as he spoke to me. "Yeah, she was with some other lady. Ran out of the restaurant a little while ago, freaking out. Maybe they had a breakup or something. The other broad is still here, enjoying some wine. You want me to tell her anything?"

"No." I wanted him to spike her drink with a few shards of silver, let Lillian get a taste of what it meant to hurt like I was. Again, I composed myself. It was a near thing. "I thank you for your time. Have a good evening."

I hung up on him and walked out to join Gabe. Together, we dug at the car and the drive, working until our clothes were freezing our sweat to us. At some point, Xavion and Leo had joined in to help. Tommy, thankfully, was fast asleep. I only hoped he wouldn't suffer through what we had.

The group of us piled into the car and I hoped it would be able to skirt along the crust of the snow. It was such a lightweight, tiny thing compared to the Hummer; and the snow hadn't completely filled my beast's tracks yet. We might make it there. If not, I'd call in a helicopter to lift us back to the house before Tommy knew we'd left. The boy would be fine left alone for a few hours. He'd...

...God, the first time I'd left him alone had led to all this. What if the pesky neighbors came over to check on us? What if they found a kid left alone in the house and he munched on them, next? No, no we had to go help Sadie. Her life was on the line. We could pay off the neighbors again if we had to.

I turned the key in the car and was met by nothing but silence.

"Oh, for fuck's sakes," Xavion snarled.

He flung himself out of the car and smacked the hood. I pulled the little lever next to my feet. Xav spent a minute or two under the hood and came back cursing at the top of his lungs. He yanked open the door and growled. "The wires to the battery have been gnawed. They're too short and there's no replacements in the house; Sadie doesn't have a damn thing to fix this car besides a jump box. That isn't going to do it."

"So, we just sit here and hope she pops up?" Leo said, incredulous.

Xav's shoulders slumped. "There's nothing else we can do. A chopper takes time and-"

My phone rang and I eyed it. The name displayed across the front was the one person I wanted to speak to the least.

"Hudson, I'm afraid your new pet has run off into the night. She may be just a little insane," Lillian said without waiting for me to answer.

I stifled a snarl of my own. "And how did you know I was asking?"

"Do you think that I don't have ears everywhere? You called the kitchen. They came out to ask me about her. It wasn't particularly difficult to put together. Now, maybe for someone like you-"

"What did you do?" I grated.

She met me with a cascade of laughter, the sort of sinister shit you'd have expected from a cartoon supervillain on Saturday mornings. I clenched my teeth and tried not to smash my phone. Eventually, she answered. "I gave her a drink a friend of mine found out about in Asia. He'd gotten too close to the humans during the Moon and, oopsie. Rather than relying on the justice of the local supernatural order, he found some old fae mage in the hills and they created the recipe together. Thankfully, the ingredients are easy to find. You'll never have her again."

"Where is she?"

"Does it matter? She's just some stupid little human now. You've never cared for them before, why would you now?" Lillian paused, then purred at me. "Do you love her, Hudson? Did you want to spend the rest of eternity with her in your pack, hunting stupid, defenseless sheep until you both got shot?"

The rage left me in a terrible swoop. Tears touched my cheeks. "Did you hurt her?"

"Oh, goodness. Are you *crying*?" She sounded delighted. "I should have set her on fire, rolled her corpse out into traffic, and sent you the pictures. She ran away from me before I could do that. You should have seen her face when she realized she couldn't feel any of you anymore."

The growls of my pack mates echoed throughout the tiny car. I hung up on the hateful old bitch and tried Sadie's phone again; once, twice, three times.

Gabe jerked his head around as headlights poured onto the house from around the corner. The Hummer dragged its way into the driveway, its movement stiff and uncertain, as though it wasn't sure it was in the right place. The four of us were on it the moment it stopped. I ripped open the door and Sadie fell out into my arms, smelling like acid and dogsick.

It didn't matter. We rushed her into the house, taking care not to bump her head on the entryway around the door or anything like that. She murmured, but I couldn't make out what she was saying. My phone was lost in the shuffle, getting her onto the couch inside and wrapping a blanket around her. She was ice cold to the touch.

I looked back at Leo. "See if she had the heat on. It should still be warm out there."

"Got it," he said, and was gone.

My hands cupped her face, trying to warm her up. I crawled onto the couch with her, drew her into my arms, and held her tight. Being close to her without being able to really feel her hurt like walking across hot coals, but Sadie's lips had a blue tinge to them that I hated. What if Lillian's stupid potion had poisoned her? I couldn't imagine some mage working with the stuff you got at the grocery store and I wouldn't put it past her to fuck up something that was supposedly so simple.

Sadie stirred against me and sighed. "Xav...?"

She didn't even know who I was. I had skin-to-skin contact with her and she didn't realize it was me. It would have been one thing if we'd been surrounding her, if she had the whole pack wrapped around her at one time, but Xavion had followed Leo. I was the only one near her at the moment.

"No. No, it's Hudson. Did you have the heat on in the car? What happened at the restaurant?" I tried not to demand too much from her, but my voice came out in a gruff half-snarl that made her flinch away from me.

"Take it easy with her," Gabe whispered.

I turned to him and searched his face for some reassurance. I couldn't lose another mate, not Sadie, not now. We'd been a complete pack, happy and comfortable. We'd made love, all of us at once. We'd even marked her already, showing the werewolf world that she was *ours*.

Gabe shook his head and I looked at her neck. The skin was pale, sickly, but untouched. My chin quivering, I turned her head to the side and saw nothing where Gabe's mark had been.

Xavion followed Leo in, but it was Xav who spoke up. "Heat wasn't on. Doesn't smell right in there, either. Like astringent, or like those hospitals that reek of cleaner and death. Does she need a doctor?"

"No."

Sadie's eyes opened as she spoke. Her color was a little better, but nowhere near what I wanted it to be. She cleared her throat and spoke again. "No doctors. Nobody but us. I don't know what she did to me. She ruined it. She ruined it all."

"She didn't ruin a damned thing," Gabe snapped. "And you don't worry about her. You rest, you recover. We should have never let you go."

Our little omega sighed and those eyes slid shut again. "Wanted to go. Wanted to try to save us."

And she was out like a light. I slid my arms under her and carried her to the bedroom. Gabe went to check on Tommy as the rest of the pack joined me in the guest room. There was a bigger bed there, thicker blankets, more comfortable pillows. Like everything else, Sadie gave her all to those who depended on her and left herself wanting.

I put her down in that big bed and slid right in with her. Gabe rejoined me, Xavion and Leo following close by. The four of us crept into bed with her, curling up under the covers to keep warming her up. Her breath smelled like alcohol and I assumed that Lillian had gotten her pretty drunk before Sadie had run away. I didn't approve of drunk driving, but then, who did?

But I understood that it'd been a panicked moment and there was no damage to the Hummer. She'd had to escape, knowing what she knew when she lost her connection with us. And she'd come back to her pack as fast as she could, looking for solutions and finding just... us.

"No one leaves tonight," I said. "Even if she's up and feeling better, we stay with her. Vengeance can wait until another day."

Xavion glared at me. "If I want to go tear her head off, I'll go do it."

"And leave us as three to face judgment from the others?" Gabe asked. "We need you. We all need the pack to remain intact. Sadie isn't with us anymore." He saw my face and amended it. "Not like that, anyway. There's nothing we can do about that until we get permission."

The thought had crossed my mind. It would be nothing to simply turn her again, but the Meet would find a werewolf, not a human. And what if Lillian told them about her creative solution to Sadie's new furry problem? They would expect to find her human, not part of the pack, and they'd know what I'd done. One accidental turning by a pup had the slightest chance of being forgiven.

If I went against the cultural rules that I'd been raised with, ignored the statutes and the regulations set down by those who had come decades before us, there would be no mercy. And it was likely that, after getting my first mate killed with some stupid sheep, they would judge us to be so impossible to control that we would all have to be euthanized.

It would, of course, be for the greater good. Isn't that usually the theme with idiots like that? We'll take care of you until you screw up, but then it's time to kill you; for the greater good. These kids? A problem. Kill them for the greater good.

So many creatures, human and non-human alike, had died for the ever-mysterious greater good, and the goddamned world just got worse.

"It's a good plan," Leo said, finally. "We stay with her. And when we go to the Meet, we present her as a human desperate to get back to her pack. Maybe Lillian just gave us the help we needed."

I shot him a glare. "I doubt it. It's more likely that they'll force us to leave her as she is. They'll have her memories destroyed by one of their psychics."

"Do the tarot card flippers really have powers?"

Gabe shrugged. "Some of them do. Whether they know it or not is a completely different story. Regardless, everyone has their own magic. Even we do."

"But we don't get into people's heads," Leo frowned. "We just do that wolf thing. And sometimes we make ourselves a little more invisible."

My fingers ran through Sadie's hair. "But their people can do that, Leo. And if their people can do that to her, what do you think they can do to us? Would death be worse than forgetting all of this ever happened?"

The pack fell silent at that, glances exchanged, discomfort evident on their faces. I didn't want to frighten them worse than that, but it gave them plenty to think about. If there were members of our society capable of doing such things, I had little doubt that it had happened before.

It was the sort of thing that made you doubt what you really knew. Sure, your reality was what you remembered; but what if someone had fucked around with it?

Sadie stirred in my arms and the pack, as one, scooted closer to her. Her cheeks held a touch of pink in them, her lips closer to her normal color than the blue-tinged tone that had me on edge. My nerves settled a little. In a week, we would be at the Meet no matter what happened. Sadie wasn't going to go anywhere, no matter what we had to do. And it was likely that our stubbornness was going to lead to our downfall, no matter how much we protested.

I'd told her that she was ours, that we took care of our own. That hadn't changed and, as I looked around at my pack, I knew they felt the same.

Even if it meant total ruin, we were going to save our mate.

Chapter 16
Sadie

I spent most of the week in bed, Bosco or Lady asleep beside me when the pack wasn't occupying it. When I got up, the others treated me as if I were as fragile as glass. Was it that way when werewolves and humans fell in love? Were the wolves always worried that they might hurt a human like me?

Never had I hated being what I was. I'd been human nearly my entire life, but the taste of something new, something different, had excited every sense I had. It'd also added a few senses to me, expanding my mind and ensnaring my imagination. I tried to come to terms with the fact that I was just a plain old human again, but nothing really stuck.

And everything sucked.

It didn't matter what I did; the guys did it for me. I was practically a prisoner in my own house. Though they kept assuring me that I could do what I wanted, after I'd gotten up, it always felt like they were five steps ahead of me. Going to feed the dogs? They'd already done it. Trying to go change the cat litter boxes? No, that'd been done that morning. Two days in a row I'd thrown out perfectly good litter, not realizing that they'd taken care of it much earlier than I was used to.

Not that we didn't have plenty of litter around these days. Every single bag was proudly marked with the Fontaine Feeds logo. In a time when I wanted control of myself, I had control of absolutely nothing.

I knew they were just trying to be kind, but it was too much to cope with all at once.

The moon began Her ascent early that evening, right around six. Hudson had explained that the full moon wouldn't actually occur until nearly midnight, but when it happened their transformations would be forced. None of them were certain what would happen to me, if anything did. They'd never known a werewolf who had been turned into a human.

We took the Hummer, just in case we actually made it back. My stomach fizzed with discomfort and I wanted to be anywhere else other than the Judgment Grounds the Meet would be held on. They were due north of my house, about six miles, as far into the wilderness as you could get without heading out of our area.

I wondered how many trials had happened without my knowledge. How many people had been killed or excommunicated, their lives in ruin while I slept warm and cozy in my bed? Mind you, that happened everywhere. When I'd lived in the city, you didn't feel any different when someone got mugged half a mile from your house. It didn't change your night if they got shot or ended up dead in the hospital.

But the danger had been one of the reasons I'd been so excited to head back to the country, escaping the crushing enclosure of civilization for somewhere a hell of a lot quieter. Look at where that had gotten me.

The Hummer turned down a nearly invisible little trail, as hard to find as the one that opened to one side of my house. We went down, deep into the forest, and I twitched when Hudson turned off the headlights.

"The dragons don't care for lights like this in the dark. Hurts their eyes. Eskal, the head of their flight, is likely to be the tie-breaking vote tonight. Better to play it nice," he said.

Xavion snorted. "More likely that we'll see heads roll if he's the deciding factor. I think he's in Lil's pocket."

Hudson nearly clipped a tree. Gabe glared at Xavion but I moved between them, shushing them. I understood why they were so irritable. Not only were they taking me in for potential execution, but the kid strapped to his car seat was under investigation, too. And it felt so wrong to trap him in a seat, drag him out into the woods, and threaten his tiny life.

I had to remind myself that my favorite fantasy books often bound children only a little older than Tommy to oaths and wretched futures. And those books killed those kids without a second thought, too. Still, it was different when it was a child I loved rather than words on a page. If we didn't all make it out of this, I wondered if I'd ever be able to read those books again.

A clearing deep in the woods had other vehicles already in it. The moon was a bright, full circle above our heads as Hudson parked and we got out. I took Tommy in my arms and kissed the top of his human head. He yawned, nestled into my chest, and caught the moon out of the corner of his eye. He went rigid, his pupils widening like dinner plates. I stroked his back and followed my silent pack mates... my... no, they were. I followed my silent pack mates to whatever future lie before us.

We walked across a bridge that crossed a small brook, pausing only to let a silver-haired young man run some sort of burning herbs around us. He smiled sadly at Tommy and placed his hand atop the boy's head momentarily, mouthing a mantra or a prayer. Then he looked up at me and said, "May you only find joy in these coming hours."

"A-and you?" I said, confused.

He bowed his head and let us through.

If I hadn't spent the past month among werewolves, I would have ended up on my knees at what I saw.

Dragons walked past us, the size of motorhomes, as varied as a jewelry case. Unicorns galloped by in groups, tossing their manes and all but glittering beneath the moon. Big cats that belonged on the savannah lay together in a pride, each with their paws wrapped around a chunk of meat the size of my head. Their faces were covered in blood, the occasional droplet falling from their chins, but they didn't seem to notice.

The trees were alive with griffins, their heads tucked beneath their wings as they waited for the night's problem to be solved. I hadn't considered that there would be diurnal creatures at the Meet, but I supposed not everything could be the kind of stuff that went bump in the night.

Maybe they were right to ban people like me from their secret society. I could barely cope with the understanding of what I was seeing, but my alphas looked as if they had expected even more visitors of a supernatural nature. I reached back and took Gabe's hand. He squeezed it in turn and pulled me closer to the pack's protection.

"Aunnie!"

Tommy squirmed in my arms, wiggled out of them, and scampered over to Lillian. She was dressed all in crimson, looking like she'd been rolling in blood. She gasped and grabbed the boy, picking him up and hugging him tight. Hudson was there before I could stop it from happening. He snarled at her and stole his son back, his eyes changing to that of a wolf in a second flat.

The clearing was as silent as the grave, all eyes on the two of them. I beat a path over to them and, carefully, extracted Tommy from Hudson's arms. Then I hurried back to the safety of the rest of the pack, leaving Hudson to do whatever it was he felt was necessary. I sure wasn't about to intrude on a family matter.

"If the wolves in question will come to order," sighed a baritone voice.

In those few moments, the moon had risen enough to illuminate a long, flat stone shelf upon the ground. There, a dragon sat nearly as tall as the trees, staring down at us. His scales were as dark as the night sky, picked out with pinpricks of light. He was a mirror image of the stars above, with a crescent moon upon his brow. Molten pools of gold gazed down at me in particular and the wind left my lungs.

I turned so Tommy wouldn't have to deal with the power bearing down on us. Instead, my puppy flailed for his aunt and completely ignored the dragon.

"Mmnph," said the dragon. He snorted, then addressed the rest of the clearing. "I, Eskal of the Nightflight, bring this Meet to order. If I may have representatives of our communities to act in judgment join me, please."

While it wasn't a request so much as a command, at least someone had drilled manners into his head at some point. A griffin floated down to land beside him. A lion padded up to flop down beside the griffin and I watched as a unicorn, all regal majesty, meandered up to the stone.

Standing there like that, looking down at my werewolves and I, I got the impression that the lion couldn't have cared less. Maybe they were werecats and they'd experienced the same sort of problems in the past. The unicorn seemed only to want to come and visit us.

I worried about the griffin and the dragon, both of which focused directly on me.

"Proceed," the dragon said, tilting his head at Lillian.

Lillian stepped forward and spread her hands. "All I want is to clear my nephew of the atrocity his father allowed him to commit. Perhaps he even encouraged him to do it. My friends, you know I am a good and true wolf. I have protected our society throughout the years, but Hudson?" She rolled her eyes. "A human stands among us because of his lack of responsibility. Who knows how damaging she could be? I recommend the extermination of her and the rest of the pack. I would take my nephew under my wing and assure he never causes a problem again."

"If it wasn't for you, I'd be here as a werewolf," I snapped without thinking.

That enormous dragon looked back at me and I flinched, waiting for that terrible surge of power. This time, it didn't come. "Explain."

"Tommy, the pup in my arms, bit me when he got lost from his folks. He got stuck in a dog trap," I said, daring to look up at that massive scaley head. "I work in animal rescue, you see, and when he got stuck in a dog trap my neighbors had set out, I had to help him. It was cold. He was scared. And I knew he didn't belong with them. He nipped me, drew blood, and Hudson and the others showed up to set it to rights."

The dragon glanced at my pack as I continued, changing the story so Gabe wouldn't get in trouble. "But I freaked out. I shapeshifted and I ended up under Tommy's crib. They thought they couldn't change me back after that and, your honor-" I hesitated. Were you supposed to call a dragon that? "...Mr. Nightflight? I was happy. I was happier than I've ever been and..."

My voice stuck in my throat and I had to turn away from him. A line of tears rolled down either my cheeks. "I had a family. I was so happy. And I just want that back, please. If you'd give them permission to do it this time, I'd be really grateful. They're all I want, and I promise, I'll do whatever I have to and keep all this a secret. I wouldn't want any of you to be hurt. You're all too amazing for that."

"And so, how are you human again, o great savior of mortal beasts?" sneered the griffin.

I turned my attention to him and shrugged. "I don't really know, sir. Lillian invited me out to a restaurant and she spiked my drink with something. I don't know what it was. But it nearly killed me and it hurts so much to be disconnected from my pack, I-"

"You attacked your own guest?"

The dragon's attention locked on Lillian, who was paler than the snow around us. I blinked and looked back at the alphas near me. Hudson, who had rejoined us, had an expression of realization on his face. He stepped forward. "She did. She poisoned Sadie."

"It was hardly poison," Lillian protested, stepping back from the stone. "But she wasn't one of us, she didn't need to be one of us to be here."

"You poisoned your own guest in a public place," the dragon stated, walking toward Lillian. "A place that could have endangered the humans present, killed this woman, and exposed us all to a cataclysmic amount of humanity."

He stopped when he was a few feet away from her, smoke curling from his nostrils. "What did you give her?"

"Emperweed," Lillian whispered, shrinking beneath him.

The smoke increased tenfold. "A plant known for its toxicity. You attempted to murder one of your own kind rather than bring her to justice."

"No!" Lillian cried, spreading her hands wide. "No, I was told it would just reverse the change in her. There was a small chance it could hurt her but- Eskal, you have to understand. Hudson killed my little sister, he doesn't-"

The dragon's eyes narrowed as he interrupted her. "Doesn't deserve to be happy. You pull the Meet into a family matter of jealousy, nearly kill the woman who has brought joy to your old pack, and expect us to cast them into the flames to somehow sanctify your sister's death. Becca was an idiot. She hunted soft sheep on human land. Hudson was no better but he didn't get himself killed doing it. He has atoned for his mistakes and your sister atoned with her life. But you..."

"Me?" Lillian choked. "I want justice. My nephew illegally turned-"

"I don't concern myself with a puppy's mistake when the mistake turns out to be an asset," he snapped, jaws clapping in front of her.

Each tooth was nearly as long as she was tall. I sure wasn't going to argue with that mouth.

The dragon turned, his tail smacking into Lillian and knocking her off her feet. She glared at him from the ground as he mounted the stone once more. "We must come to a consensus."

Our judges came together, speaking quietly but quickly. Lillian glared hatred at me from across the clearing, tears in her eyes. Had it really just been the potential of me replacing her sister? Was that all? People moved on from the death of a loved one, eventually, no matter how sad it was. I wasn't trying to replace the woman she'd lost, but my alphas needed an omega.

Tommy needed a mom.

I cradled him closer and turned my back on her. There was an urgency in the air, as if the supernatural beings in the area couldn't wait to get away from this Meet. I agreed with them. I wanted to go home, to bury myself in my men and make Tommy smiley-faced pancakes in the morning.

But it was possible that I never would. I held down the urge to run, to flee into the night. I had been an apex predator.

I needed to act like I deserved to be one.

"Little one. Sadie, yes?"

Eskal peered down at me from inches away. I jumped when I turned to see him so close. "Yes?"

"You wish to join our community under the guise of contentment? Do you so swear to learn the ways and necessities of it, forever keeping safe those here and those abroad?"

That sounded more positive than I'd hoped. I nodded, then realized he wanted a verbal answer. "Yes, sir. I'd never hurt any of you. I couldn't bear it. I'm sure I've got plenty to learn but I won't screw it up. I promise."

Eskal nodded, which nearly knocked me over. He sat back and looked around the clearing. "In the case of Thomas Alexander Fontaine's accident, we find the defendant innocent of all charges. Puppies make mistakes. Hudson, don't let him out of your sight until he's at least 15." He paused and I held my breath. "And do take care of this omega. She seems like a good fit."

A sob left me and I ended up on my knees, relief crippling me. I clutched Tommy to me, bowing over him, as my alphas fell around me. Arms tightened around me and I was awash in the collective scent of my pack, drowning in it, when I heard a shriek from across the clearing.

There was a bang, another, and then a second scream. I squirmed from beneath my men to stare at the chaos around me. Lillian's gun lay on the ground. Eskal had her pinned with one massive paw, his claws wrapping around her. Without another word, he took to the sky and brought her with him. Her screams echoed into the night, and, after a moment, were gone.

Slowly, the magical creatures dispersed. There was no comment on Lillian and I got the distinct impression that the dragons were sort of the lords of our community; but that they, too, were not absolved from judgment if something went wrong. I tucked myself back into my pack and waited for the others to leave.

"It's okay," Hudson whispered fifteen or so minutes later. "It's just us."

I put Tommy down and sat in the snow. He lifted his head and stared at the sky above for a moment, before falling into his puppy form. The rest of my pack shivered, though not due to the cold. Four sets of wolf's eyes stared at me, hungry and waiting.

"Kiddo," I asked, offering my hand out to Tommy. "Do you want me to be your mom?"

The pup's eyes widened. He toddled the gap between us and, well, maybe it wasn't as sweet as some may have described it, but it was plenty enough for me.

He bit me.

And I sank down into the snow, feeling the warmth seize into my veins, and found myself staring into the moon high above in the sky, a perfect circle that shed Her light down on us.

Chapter 17
Sadie

When you know what to expect, transformation doesn't hurt at all.

I breathed deep the woods around me, the pack next to me, my puppy waiting for me to join him as he pawed at my head. There wasn't the slow, lingering sense of changing so much as I was human one moment and melting fluidly into the body of a wolf the next. My dark fur was a contrast to Tommy's fluffy coat, so much so that I hoped we'd be able to find him in the snow.

I laughed at myself. What a silly notion. I pressed my snout into the pup, breathing his scent. I'd know it for the rest of my life, human or wolf. I could find him anywhere within a five-mile range.

Though it took some wiggling, I managed to get out of my clothes. Tommy, the puppy far smaller than the human boy, had slid out of his own like he was covered in grease. He barked at me, playbowed, and scampered off into the woods. I snorted and rolled to my feet, marveling in the strength of my new form and at just how right it was.

Something larger came toward me and I spun, hackles up and teeth bared. If it wanted my puppy, I would die fighting it. A low, rattling growl came from within my chest and I-

My pack looked at me like I'd cracked my head against something. I realized, other than Leo that once, I'd never seen them transformed, never known them on this level, but I recognized them on sight. Hudson, an enormous grey wolf with a scattering of black and white markings, walked up to me and nuzzled his head over mine. Gabe matched him in color, though the markings were a bit different. Leo, a tawny wolf that more or less was the same color as his human mane, danced after Tommy.

I missed Xavion the first time I looked for him. Dark as night, he blended into the shadows. My final mate came up to me and pressed his forehead to mine, his ears folding flat against his skull. Leo came up behind me and put his head on my flank. For my part, I simply breathed my pack and sighed their scent out.

The richness of alpha awakened something within me. I yearned to find a den, beg them to knot me, defend the den with my life. That den centered on our home, -our home-, back at the rescue, but any hole would work for the night. I rubbed the length of my body beneath their chins, curling my tail along Hudson's cheek. I saw him shiver, heard him groan. My jaws popped open in a pant and I looked back at them over my shoulder.

And then the hunt began.

Instinct carried me away from my pack as my heat set in. I tore through the woods, never knowing or looking at where I was going. I was powered by something I couldn't fully name, by whatever wildness had been imparted to me by the boy. When animals run through the forest, they don't stop to look for holes or roots. They simply run with the power they have, full speed and alert for dangers.

In my case, I wasn't looking for danger, exactly. There was a thrill in my heart, a sense that knew my pack was behind me and looking for me. That when they found me, all would be lost. We would go to ground somewhere out of sight, out of mind, and the world wouldn't exist for the next several hours. We could hunt for prey another night. For the time being, what they needed most was me.

My paws flew across the packed snow, light as a feather and never sinking more than an inch or two. It left a visible path for them to follow, the world a twinkling wonderland beneath Her light. I wrapped my tracks around the trees, pausing to rake my claws through the thin, weak winter bark. I exposed the greenwood beneath it in a glorious rush of ripping, tearing perfection.

I was everything humanity feared. Brilliant, powerful, and capable, I lifted my head to the night and howled my heart out.

And in the distance, my pack answered.

I waited a moment, two, then rushed off through the snow again. I twisted my path, confusing them, frustrating them. It did a man good to have to work for his catch; hell, wasn't that the whole point of courting? Make them worthy, make them find you and please you before you allowed them to take what they wanted.

A rabbit flashed across in front of me and my instincts screamed to go after it. I lunged for it, kicking up snow and dirt as I dug in. The creature screamed, igniting my predatory need. My teeth snapped an inch from its tail and it bolted down a hole, disappearing into the darkness below.

Wrinkling my nose, I began to dig. I dug in the frozen dirt until I felt the pack growing closer, so close; too close. Growling at the rabbit who had outwitted me, I ran past its burrow and hoped it would delay my alphas as it had me. A brief delay, of course. I wanted them on my tail as soon as they could manage it.

I raced through the undergrowth, letting leafless, thorny branches rip at my coat. Who cared? It only left a better trail for my alphas to follow. My scent was plenty, but the discovery of a tuft of fur would goad them on, have them drooling for me by the time they found me. And that was all I could dream of.

In the distance, I saw an opening beneath a hill. My steps slowed and I entered it, my head tilting. The faintest aroma of bear clung to it, but it wasn't deep enough for hibernation. Well sheltered, comfortable, a bed of earth and dried greenery left the perfect place for me to build. I licked my lips and walked out to find what I wanted.

Though it took me some time to construct a nest of the pine boughs and soft, fluffy antler down I'd found throughout the area, I managed it before the pack found me. I paced the front of the cavern, my tail out and alert, the tip flicking this way and that. Wherever they were, they'd stopped for some reason. Perhaps they'd found that tuft of fur.

Every salacious minute that passed made me crazier. I needed my pack, wanted them to hurry up so I could find my way to that sweet nirvana that they paved the way for. I scratched the bare dirt beneath the overhang, lifted my head, and howled again. A hunt was no fun without a climax, and I was ready for more than a few of those.

Hudson peered at me from above, standing on the overhang. He inhaled, deep and sweet, and slid down the side of the hill. His ears went back but his lips went up. I curled toward the ground, forever submissive to the alpha my heart desired. I would never challenge him over a territory like this, not when I'd brought him there.

The others came down the side after him, first Gabe, then Leo, then Xavion. At the mouth of the cave, they stared at me. However they'd told him, Tommy obeyed and stayed away from the cave yet remained within range to feel his presence. It was likely that he was simply playing, unaware that his pack was about to make me officially theirs.

I slid beneath their chins again, more cat than wolf, trying to tell them I was ready, willing, dying to be part of my pack again. I'd sworn to myself never to be that fucking goat, but God, I understood her so much more now. The need was driving me crazy and I didn't know what else I could do. I whined, arching my back against Leo's chin, just as a cloud slid across the moon.

Suddenly, I was naked and human. All of us were. Leo grabbed me around the waist with one arm and dragged me back against him. His hardness ground into my thigh and my men converged on me. I was pulled to the nest I'd made, placed upon it as if I were something cherished, and then the other shoe dropped.

If they'd been passionate with me before, this was an entirely different level. Leo kissed me, but Hudson already had his tongue between my legs. I gasped into Leo's lips as Xavion crept across me to help Hudson. The pair of them lashed me, but I was already soaked. One of my legs drew up toward my chest, trying to open myself fully to them.

And that was when Gabe sank his teeth into the side of my neck, breaking the skin and me with it. I came, the first orgasm of many promised that night, and let the silent forest know it.

There was a snarled argument at my core, my men growling at each other. I pulled away from Leo long enough to sort it out, grabbing Hudson and wrapping my arms around his neck. Without pause, his hands gripped my hips, his mouth met mine, and he slid into me as if we were made for one another.

It was when he drew away from the kiss that he snapped his jaws onto the opposite side of my neck from Gabe, where his bite had been before, copying the mark and leading me up a treacherous hill, ever pushing me toward the peak. I wrapped my legs around his hips and cried out into the snow, trying to drive him to tie me, to secure his knot and claim me.

And in time, he did. His body locked with mine, I felt his climax intermingle with my own, our bond stronger than ever. It was the cold ground beneath me, the pine needles pricking my skin, the promise of more snow in the morning, the heat of his body over mine, the breath against my neck, his tongue running over the new scars on my throat. I took all of it in, writhed, bucked, and gave in to my pack.

Gabe took me next, as soft and passionate as Hudson was fierce. Xavion, then Leo, and I took each knot one at a time. I was blind with pleasure, quivering beneath the touch of my pack as I desperately gave them all of me and brought another to heel. As Leo rested within me, his teeth high on my neck just below my ear, I tried to catch my breath.

Never in my life had I been so fulfilled, so richly exhausted by any man. Had I always needed this, a bond so passionate? I didn't know.

But it was time for round two.

Night faded into dawn and we'd exhausted ourselves. The moon had come back out, leading to more feral pleasures than my re-initiation back into the pack. And when the mating had faded, when we'd worn ourselves to the bone, Hudson and Gabe had gone out to get us a deer. They'd brought Tommy back with them and, as a family, we'd feasted until we'd been fat with the venison.

Even then my stomach growled as it continued to digest the pile of meat I'd eaten. Streaked with blood, dirt, and the various mating marks of my men, I awoke to a late morning and Gabe's arms around me. I was surrounded by my alphas, my head resting on Xavion's chest.

Hudson stood outside, naked as the day he was born, a knife busy at work butchering the deer he'd killed. I wondered, briefly, if anyone cared about us hunting in a place that wasn't ours. After all, trail cameras existed and people just loved to see what wildlife was up to these days. Had he thought of that?

"Hey," I called.

A beautiful steak in hand, he paused and looked back at me. He smiled, sending warmth rushing into me. "Hey yourself."

"There're no game cams out here or anything, right?" I returned the smile, still half asleep.

He handed the steak off to Leo and turned back to cut more meat from bone. "No, this is some kind of preserve. No one's allowed out here other than national forest people. And they're never out. We disabled the cameras years ago and have someone check up on them every few days to make sure they're still down. We can't let them get footage of us or the dragons or whomever."

"Shouldn't we be hurrying back home, just in case they show up?"

Gabe purred into my ear. "It's safe enough, love. Those few times a year that they show up, they do it during new moons. There are too many rumors, mostly from decades long-passed, about werewolves roaming these woods. People frighten easily. We encourage it with donations to keep this place human-free and spread a few rumors of our own. It was where we ran before we bought the cabin and the property."

I relaxed against him and nodded. "Did we have someone go to the house?"

"Six staff, headed out as soon as we call them. We'd never leave the rescue by itself on uncertain terms like yesterday," Hudson said.

Yesterday. The past. It was all done, all over with. I watched as he continued to work the meat from the deer's bones, Leo deftly wrapping all of it. I wondered if every month would be like this, enjoying the quiet and hiring someone to watch over the rescue for the evening. I stretched and got up, comfortable in my nudity in the open.

I'd certainly never been that cozy before becoming a werewolf. I assumed it was all part of the process. "Guys?"

My question was greeted by looks in my direction, all of them ready to jump on anything I needed.

"How often do omegas go in heat?"

Xavion shrugged. "It differs from omega to omega. Usually about once every six months, like most canids. We're derived from them, by some ritual a million years ago. Longer lifespan, though."

"I only have to deal with a period every six months?" I asked, blinking.

They looked at each other, clearly confused. Finally, Gabe said, "Well. Yeah."

"God, if that got out you guys would have women coming out of your ears."

Xavion snorted. "Too bad for them. The only girl we need is you."

It was music to my ears. I smiled at him, walked over, and kissed him. He kissed back but let me go about my business. While Gabe started a fire to cook up even more meat for breakfast, I went to find some water source to... well, wipe off in, at least. It wouldn't be a real bath, not until I got home, but I felt sticky everywhere and the whole lack of fur made me feel a little dirty.

The only water source I could find was an ankle-deep stream covered over with a thin sheet of ice. I broke through it with a rock and chipped away until I managed to get in. The water was frigid, of course, but something about the werewolf genome didn't really care about the cold. After all, I'd walked there through a snowpack of a few inches and my toes weren't even numb.

I did wonder how that would convert to hotter weather. Would we be slumped over and gasping in summer? I imagined grooming my pack and them grooming me, trying to get rid of an undercoat as fluffy and robust as the huskies back at the rescue. They required constantly undercoat raking, always producing enough coat to stuff a pillow with. Had I been the sort that spun up animal fur for clothes, I could have made a fortune off of what they naturally shed.

So many questions, never enough answers. But that didn't matter anymore. I had forever with my pack and there was always time to ask those questions, to get those answers, and to better understand who and what I was.

Once clean, I shook off and transformed back into my wolf self. The travel seemed much quicker, less of an inconvenience. Four legs were just better than two. In the middle of the forest, we ate our breakfast as a family.

And I managed to fight off the instinct to do that thing mother dogs do where they pre-chew their puppies' meals for them. But it was a close thing.

We traveled back to the Hummer, past the place where I'd last seen Lillian alive, as wolves. Her fear scent still stained the area, a rough and sour smell that was like moldy hay and lemons. I whined uncertainly and flattened my ears, hunkering my way into the car. Per usual, Hudson drove.

I was thankful for that. The only time I'd driven it, I'd ruined everything. When we got home, I was taking my old beater to the shop and never driving anything else again.

But my mind rested on Lillian. She'd been motivated by pain, not anger. I could understand that, if I wanted to. The question was; did I want to? It was hard to forgive when you were on my side of the situation, but comprehension didn't necessarily mean forgiveness.

I dithered, fighting myself with my feelings about her. What she'd done had been wrong, morally and judicially. Yet I couldn't say that, if I'd been in her shoes, that I'd have done any different.

Maybe there was some way to intercede on her behalf, still.

I shifted back to my human body and pulled my spare clothes on, thankful for the ones we'd packed in case we made it out alive. "Does anybody have Eskal's number? I want to talk to him when we get home."

Xavion handed me his phone again and I could help but wonder if I was about to start up trouble again.

Chapter 18
Gabe

As Sadie barricaded herself in her bedroom, Xav's phone at the ready, I brought my thoughts together and decided it was the perfect time to confront Hudson about an idea I'd had.

Yet, I couldn't seem to find Hudson anywhere. We'd gotten home merely an hour ago and he'd already vanished? I checked each of the bedrooms, the kennels, the various dog yards; nothing. No scent anywhere, either. Had he even come inside?

I finally found him out at the edge of the property, a wolf, marking his territory. I rolled my eyes. "Really."

He laughed at me, tongue flopping out of his mouth, and pranced over to see me. The mutt was giddy about last night, probably relieved that we hadn't gotten Sadie dead. I reached down and scratched his ears. "If you've got ten minutes, I want to make a proposal to you. One of those official ones you like so much, with different colored folders and everything."

Up went his ears. Well, that'd caught his attention. He bounded down the drive like a puppy and hurried into the house. I ran to keep up with him, my inner wolf whispering for me to change. Unlike Sadie, fresh as she was to it, we were experienced with shutting up the animal within. She'd get there, it just took time. In the meanwhile, she'd probably attack her steaks and not be the best company at a dinner table.

That was fine. We still had a couple of weeks before we intended to head back to work.

And that was why it was so important to get this out of the way.

Hudson had already pulled his pants on by the time I entered the kitchen. Bosco danced around his feet and he bent to pet the dog, who wiggled like a see-saw. I sat down across the dining table from him and tapped a stack of, as promised, multi-colored folders. "If you'd be kind enough to sit?"

My cousin made his way over and sat down in the seat I'd directed him to. "What's up?"

"It appears that we make substantial donations to rescues throughout the year, including this one. However, it also seems as though our donations are largely ignored," I said. "Essentially, we could be doing more with the money than we currently are, but we'd need to hire an expert in rescues."

I offered him the first folder, salmon in color, and tapped it. "The financial breakdown is in there."

He popped it open, looked through it, and put it to his right. "I'm listening."

"This folder," I said, picking up an aqua one, "Contains current metrics for sustainable rescues around the country. There are a great many of them that do transport services, too, getting dogs and cats from overrun shelters to areas where they're more likely to be adopted. There's also a fiscal breakdown there, too."

He frowned at the folder and looked between the two. I saw the realization take him. "You want to hire Sadie."

"I mean," I held up the remaining folders; a denim, an indigo, and an ebony. "If you didn't get it before I got through all of the folders, I was going to write each letter that began each color and literally spell it out for you."

"You're color-coding your business proposals? Like *that*? That's shockingly subtle of you."

I grinned at him. "She's been running this little place for ages. She's incredibly successful, there's just not a lot of donation power out here. I think we can build a better shelter system than the one currently in place in most areas. And I think she's the key to that. Imagine, Fontaine Feeds not only sponsors shelters; we build them. We make the world a safer, happier place for pets everywhere. And it all starts with her."

"She'd be tickled pink. Salmon," Hudson said, tapping the salmon pink folder in front of him. "It'd stop her from getting all upset every time we buy something for her, too. She'd be able to run rescues all over the country with our money without having to worry about taking it from us. It'd just be a resource for her. And the PR campaigns would be incredible for... everything."

Leaning back in my chair, I put my hands behind my head. "I'm a genius, the best business mind you've ever met, smartest guy in the world. Et cetera. Lay it on me."

Hudson got up and stacked the folders together once more. "You are. And I see no reason why she wouldn't accept. We can stay in the area, she can help every animal she wishes to, and we keep the company running at full speed. It's perfect."

"Think I should go bother her? I can't imagine Eskal is taking that long to talk to her."

He nodded and I got up, taking my folders with me. Sadie would want to see the figures, even if I had to explain a few for her. It'd turned out that she was some kind of wizard with math, making money out of thin air when she'd needed to pay for a dog's surgery or a cat's neuter.

I understood that. How many times had we managed to keep our finances in check, even when it felt like there was no way to do it? We'd run up a few credit cards, but it hadn't been anything we couldn't take care of the moment Fontaine Feeds had hit its stride.

Sadie's door was still closed. I put my ear against it and listened, but didn't hear her talking. I gave it a gentle rap with my knuckles and waited. Invading my mate's personal space was too rude even for me.

...And I continued to wait. After a few minutes, I peeked inside to find her fast asleep. She'd had a long day, a longer night; which I remembered with relish, and I had no doubt that she needed some downtime. Be that as it was, I stepped inside and closed the door behind me. I needed to know if she was interested. If she wasn't, I needed time to find other candidates.

"Whaa?" she asked as I shook her shoulder.

I sat down on the bed beside her. "It's me, honey. Wake up. I need to talk to you about something."

As soon as I said it, I flinched. There were better ways to phrase such things, ones that didn't make it sound like you were about to step on someone's heart. She woke up plenty fast after that and up she sat, eyes owlish with worry. "Did I do something wrong? You guys aren't mad at me, are you?"

"Never. But I did have something I wanted to go over with you."

I ran my fingers through her hair, down and cupping her cheek. Just touching her sent little shivers of delight running up my arm. I put the folders down and drew her close. If she wanted evidence, she could pick them up. She turned her head up to me and blinked. "Most of the time, if people stall, it's a bad thing."

"There's a chance you might not like it."

Her brows creased. "Might not like it?"

"I spoke with Hudson," I said, my fingers disappearing beneath the hem of her shirt and starting an upward journey. My lips touched her neck. I was usually professional, but I wanted to devour her. "We want to make you an offer."

"An offer? Gabe, if you start all your offers this way, I'm going to be incredibly jealous when you go back to work."

I chuckled. "Only for gorgeous werewolf women."

"I'm listening," she said, smiling.

My hands came to rest on her belly, beneath her clothes. "We want you to head a division of Fontaine Feeds, The Fontaine Foundation. It deals with rescue across the world, intent on finding homes for those animals who are displaced by fortune or failure. You've done an incredible job here. I think it's time you take your career to the next level."

"My career?" Sadie whispered. "No one's ever called it that before. Most people around here mock me or expect me to take whatever wanders on to their property. And I do, but that's beside the point."

I tilted my head at her. "You have a passion for securing the lives of the small, though often in furry form. You were driven to save Tommy and the rest of us, not just because you loved us, but because you're terrible at tolerating injustice. You'd be an asset to Fontaine Feeds, and I think you'd be a perfect fit. This isn't just because we love you, Sadie. It's because you're the right person for the role."

"And then I can't complain about all of you blowing money on rescue if I'm the one managing it."

Grinning, I nipped her ear. "I suppose there's that, too, but it's the company's money. Not ours. We just take our pay from it."

"If you're sure no one will mind or there's no one better to do it, I'm all for it," she said, squirming to tuck herself beneath my chin.

"They won't. Honestly, the office probably won't even bother you after the first week or two. They'll want to feel you out, meet who stole our hearts, and try to understand your purpose. After that? They'll settle right in with you." I paused, then peeked down at her. "Why did you want to make a call, anyhow?"

"I don't know if it'd make sense."

"You can try me?"

Sadie sighed and looked out the window across from us. "I want to try to help Lillian. Maybe the big, scary dragon hasn't eaten her yet. I don't know. But I don't think it's fair that she gets fried or whatever was going to happen to us. She had an honest problem with me. She tried to solve it herself. Maybe she did it wrong, but people tend to overreact."

"She tried to kill you and missed the dose. Sadie, she wanted to use you to punish Hudson for her sister. That's it," I said, alarmed. I couldn't let Sadie go running off, maybe try to rescue Lil. She was gone. The problem was over. That was the end of the story.

But she continued as though I hadn't spoken. "I mean, if someone came in and decided to play mom to my nephew, I'd want to get to know her. I'd probably be defensive, too. I'd be irritable and I'd absolutely blame someone like Hudson for what happened, even if it was stupid to do it. And don't get me wrong, I do think it's stupid. But it feels like I'm being haunted by the ghost of someone I never met. I owe it to Becca, if I'm going to take her place as your omega, as Tommy's mom, to make sure that Lillian doesn't die because of me."

"That's noble, I suppose, Sadie, but you can't change the past. You aren't responsible for it," I told her.

She shook her head. "I know I'm not, but Eskal is going to reconsider what he wanted to do with her. I was hoping that maybe there was some kind of testimony I could give. Like maybe if I said I didn't want her dead, he'd do something else with her."

"He might," I agreed. "You already talked to him?"

"As much as I could. Mostly, he just listened."

I nodded. "Then that's as much as you can do. I'm sure he'll be back to you in a day or two. But she tried to kill you. Humans wouldn't tolerate attempted murder, either."

"I suppose not," Sadie said, her shoulders slumping. "But we need a bigger impact on the supernatural world. The dragons can't have this much control over it, no matter what."

"Are you suggesting some kind of coup?"

"I don't know what I'm suggesting, but I know that I don't want Tommy bound to laws like we have now. What if it's his son or daughter that does what he did? What if that omega doesn't react the way I did?"

Frowning, I wound that around in my mind. Werewolves are not forward thinkers or long-term planners, for the most part. The business was a different thing altogether, but we still encouraged the use of financial planners and human thinktanks to prepare some of our proposals for us. Though we were perfectly capable wolves, it was sometimes difficult to think beyond the current status of our lives.

It was just part of how things worked when some of your mind was shared with someone who liked to dig holes and flush squirrels out of the brush.

The idea of Tommy suffering what we'd worried would befall us was too much. And Sadie had a point; why did the dragons have final say over what happened? They'd been contested now and then, but maybe we were being rolled onto our backs when it wasn't really appropriate.

"It's something to talk to Hudson about, see what he thinks. Until then, we'll wait and see what Eskal does. And we'll get you ready to head to your first day at work. How about that?"

She blinked at me. "Are there things I need to know before we go back to work? Like, weird social werewolf billionaire things?"

I laughed and began to explain the internal hierarchy of Fontaine Feeds. We spent most of the afternoon there, talking and helping her figure out how she would perform her role. And, to be honest, it was nice to get back to work. I'd craved something different, had a taste of it, and was ready to go back to our old normal plus Sadie. She'd been the final piece in our puzzle, what we needed to make Fontaine Feeds special; and our personal life, too.

And she was smart as a whip. She found flaws in my plans, small ones that we spent time correcting. We were nearly finished when Xav's phone rang. Sadie was on it in an instant.

"Hello?" she answered.

I could hear someone on the other end and, after a moment, recognized Eskal's voice. I didn't interrupt, not wanting to set the dragon off if he'd considered her request. Sadie's face fell as she listened and it was as if someone had punched me in the gut.

When she hung up, she sighed and looked down at the phone. I reached out and put my hand over it. "You tried your best. She would have never advocated for you, if she'd been in your shoes."

"He's going to exile her to another city that's willing to take on an alpha female in their pack," she said.

I stared at her. "She's getting a reset?"

"Is that what you call it? A reset?"

I withdrew my hand from the phone and put it in my lap. "It's not really what we call it, but it's what we've always called it around here. I didn't think he'd do it."

"What can I say?" Sadie said, smiling at me. "I guess I'm a miracle worker."

"She doesn't deserve it."

"I know."

"She'd have killed you as easily as watching you breathe."

"It isn't about that."

Watching her smile widen, I wasn't certain I'd ever understand what it was really about. Maybe she had been plagued by a ghost, or maybe our new mate just had a conscience made of gold. I sighed and kissed her forehead. "Becca would have loved you."

Dinner that night was all excitement and discussion about Sadie's new role in the company. I thought I'd seen my packmates enthused about new packaging or new formulas of feed, but this was a thousand times that. We spent every night thereafter working with her, helping her learn what to say and how to speak to those who were under her. There was always a chance that subordinates may try to fight back against a newcomer and we wanted to prepare her for it.

Yet, by the night before our grand return to the company, Sadie sounded as if she'd been with us from the start. She was passionate, endearing, and daring; the three things that any good high-ranking businessperson needed to be.

Besides that, it'd be good for her to get away from the house now and then. The rescue would continue to have a solid support staff, though I assumed that Sadie would want to expand it in the near future. Maybe we'd spend the spring building outdoor enclosures for the birds, giving them more room to fly. We could always heat the buildings and, sadly, there always seemed to be a great deal of exotic parrots with no homes and few rescues taking them in.

We took her to work with us the following day and peeked in on her now and then, making sure that there was nothing she needed. I stopped by her new office just before the staff went home and leaned on her doorframe.

Sadie was at work on a grant request, already trying to spend money other than ours. From a selfish point of view, it was a wonderful idea.

From a logical standpoint, it was more work than she needed to expend. "You can just use the money put in the account, you know."

Her head popped up and she smiled at me. She was adorable in a comfortable pantsuit of midnight blue. "I know that, but I want to have a backup just in case. Besides, I'm diverting all of this directly to a different kind of rescue."

"Oh?"

"There's a wolf sanctuary up north that keeps wolves and wolf dogs from being put down in shelters when they're too dangerous to be adopted out. They take them all in and let them loose on several hundred acres of land." The smile turned into a grin. "It only seemed right for us to help them out."

Too right it did.

Chapter 19
Hudson

"Are you sure you want to do this?"

I felt as though I were questioning her at every step. Most women would have been frustrated, to say the least. Not Sadie. After years of dealing with animals that worried about every choice, she was used to questions.

And she was getting used to reassuring my stupid, barky brain.

She smiled back at me. "I'm positive. It's going to be okay. But we're going to be late. Come on."

Winter was in full swing but the Hummer had made the trek to the courthouse easily enough. I glanced at the parking lot and spotted Lillian's car. The need to growl at it was fierce, overwhelming, but I managed to hold it in. Distracted by it, Sadie took me by the hand and tugged me toward the building.

Eventually, I followed.

"Your plans in Omaha are going well, I hear," I murmured to her as we walked past active court sessions.

Sadie's hand tightened on mine, an affectionate squeeze. "We've got vets lined up around the block trying to seek employment at the new shelters. It's a full-time gig and they don't have to try to advertise a personal clinic. Turns out that most of them hate trying to establish themselves. Who'd have thought it?"

"Who dave foght it," echoed Tommy as he toddled along the yellowing tiles.

She beamed down at him. "That's right. Whoda thought it? Can't imagine that people aren't going to stand up and take notice of you guys now, right?" Her head turned back toward me and I saw her squinting. "Who are you again? Fountain... something?"

"Hilarious," I deadpanned.

Her eyes sparkled. There was a little snap of excitement through our connection, the close quarters making certain that I felt everything she did and vice versa. We paused at the end of the hallway. The double oak doors held our future behind it, another judgment that would set in motion an entire lifetime of differences. I glanced at her, checking one last time, but she'd already let go of Tommy's hand to push open one of the doors. She held it for my son and then, gently, pulled me through it.

I hadn't spent extra to be first in line, we'd simply been the first in alphabetical order. The three of us walked into the court and sat down on the first bench. The judge entered and we rose, waiting until we were told to sit once more. Tommy was thoroughly overexcited by the entire process and the judge, a beta werewolf from a different pack, smiled down at him.

The court case was quick. I was asked a handful of questions. Sadie was asked another handful. It slowed a little when Sadie called Lillian as her character witness, but Lillian did as she'd promised and told the court about her apprehension; and what had won her over in the end.

Of course, she didn't bring up dragons. Those don't exist. But her mention of Sadie correcting problems for her with no personal gain seemed to win over the judge. Perhaps he was aware of what had happened to Tommy's birth mother. Perhaps not. Word often traveled quickly within the supernatural community, but those listeners often found it unreliable.

"Ms. Adelaine, if you'd sign here," one of the court helpers asked, offering Sadie a form.

She filled it out quickly and handed it to me. There was a spot for me to sign and, last but not least, Lillian. I signed and eyed Lillian as I offered it to her.

Lillian, for her part, completely ignored me. She signed the paper, nodded in our general direction, and gave it back to the clerk. Then she got up and left the room.

The judge made the announcement to the room, but I didn't care. I pulled Sadie and Tommy close, hugging the boy between us. We'd walked into family court as a family to begin with. Just because adoption papers had been signed, finalized, and announced to those in attendance, made no difference. It was just more convenient when dealing with the overwhelming human population at large.

It always struck me as a little ironic that another werewolf had made that announcement.

Tommy chattered to his new, official mom as we walked back through the courthouse. I paid the minuscule paperwork fee at the desk near the exit, then gathered my mate and our son and headed into the wide, open world together.

Only one tiny detail made it a misery.

Lillian.

She waited by her car, watching us walk out. Sadie walked toward her, but I took Sadie's wrist and kissed the top of her hand. "Get Tommy in the Hummer. I'll be back in just a minute. I'd rather you not be anywhere near her, given what she did the last time you were within arm's reach."

I watched as my omega argued with herself over whether or not to argue with *me*. After a brief disagreement internally, she sighed and went to strap our boy into his car seat. I strode over to Lillian and, had I been in my true body, my hackles would have been up. "I appreciate you doing what you did in there."

"I said I would," Lillian frowned. I'd caught her off guard with the gratitude. Good.

"You've said a lot of things over the years," I said, then leaned against the car next to hers. "I still don't get it. But Sadie does, and that's the important thing. She saved your life. You gave her your family. I'd call that square, wouldn't you?"

Lillian glared at me, held eye contact for a moment, then sighed and looked away. "I suppose it's square enough."

"Does visitation help?"

She stilled for a solid 10-count. Then she looked at me once more. "Visitation?"

"One weekend a month, at your leisure. You can bank them if you want, so you can get a week with the little guy here and there. You're invited to holidays, full moons, and things like his birthday or his first day of school. The guys and I were against it because of what you did to her. Hell, we didn't even want her to call Eskal for you and, had we known that's what she was doing, we may have tried to stop her. But she did it and you're still Tommy's aunt. She insists."

Lillian swallowed and lowered her head. "Maybe she's an all right omega after all."

It was the best I'd get out of her under the current circumstances. I inhaled and narrowed my eyes. Sorrow rolled off of Lillian, masked by her usual flowery perfume. Maybe Sadie was right. I'd lost, mourned, and healed from Becca's death; but what had I really done to assure Lillian did the same for her sister?

I'd spent money, but that wasn't the only thing that mattered in life.

"Lil."

She sniffled.

"I'm sorry I wasn't there for you when Becca died." It was a stiff, brittle apology that withered as I said the words, but it was honest.

A couple of tears rolled down her cheek. She rubbed at them, trying to hide the fact that she had feelings. After all, how dare she; right? "You just don't understand. It was so hard. We were raised together. She was my other half. She knew everything about me." Lillian paused and scrubbed at her face again, ashamed of just being... well.

Not human, but you know what I mean.

After a second's pause, I drew her into my arms and held her as I had at the funeral. There, she'd punched me in the face and screamed at me to leave her alone. She'd said she wasn't interested in someone like me. I hadn't so much as tried to make a move; the feeling was mutual.

And that, as much as Becca's death, had been the start of our feud.

It'd taken Sadie coming into my life to show me how stupid it was. I nestled Lillian's hair and shushed her as she cried, letting her get it all out at last. After all, she was pack. Perhaps she didn't fall directly under me nor was she my equal, but she was pack in an extended sense. It was unlikely that she would drive so far just to hunt with us under full moons, but one never knew what could happen.

We had eternity, unless something killed us directly. I was sure we'd work it out.

"I should let you get back to your pack," she whispered, pulling away. "I'm sorry. I don't mean to be such a weakling."

I rolled my eyes and hugged her again, a bear hug this time. "Don't be silly. Call. Make appointments nearby. Stop by just to chat. It'll take time for us to work through the past couple of years, but I think it's worth the effort."

"Yeah?"

"Yeah."

Lillian shook her head at me and climbed into her car without another word. I moved back so she could pull out of the parking space, turn around, and leave. I watched her go, thoughtfully, and turned a few ideas over in my head as she disappeared into the traffic of the city.

"Hudson, kiddo says he's starving. He could eat a whole moose," Sadie called.

She wiggled her brows at me when I looked at her. I laughed and shook my head. Given the chance, I had no doubt he probably could. I walked back to the Hummer, got inside, and headed to the nearest McDonald's to grab the kid a Happy Meal. It only seemed appropriate on such a happy day.

Traffic was a brief, passing irritation. I had my family with me and the rest of the pack at home. We hadn't been back to the mansion in what felt like forever and I'd placed it up for sale the other day. There was no point in keeping it. We didn't intend to return to that life.

Instead, I pulled through the Secret Garden-esque flair of the driveway and headed into the parking area. The others had brought their vehicles by now, each of us parking down the lane as necessary. We'd had it widened so we could do three-point turns to get out. Sadie didn't mind, so long as we were careful with the local wildlife.

That had cost approximately $300,000 when we'd discovered a rare type of bird nesting in the trees, completely off-season. But that's a story for another day.

Fucking phoenixes.

Xavion met us at the door, a grin on his face. "I've got an idea."

"Oh, no," I said, deadpanning him, too.

He shoved me, snorting. "Don't be such a dick. You guys get the adoption paperwork finalized?"

Sadie held up a folder and waved it at him. "He's all mine."

"Good, we need a lady's touch with that kid," Xavion said. "Get in here. We've got a huge proposal for both of you to see. Leo's been screwing around with Powerpoint all day long. It looks great."

I tilted my head at him, forever half a dog, even as a person. I held the door open for Sadie and Tommy, following the pair of them into the house. The cake we'd ordered to celebrate Tommy's adoption stood 3 tiers tall on the table, the frosting well set in the cool room. Xavion led us into the former living room. We'd dubbed it the Decision Den, because it seemed as though the computers and work ended up in the room no matter how much we tried to keep it out.

Live like a pack, work like a pack, I guess.

Gabe had linked Leo's laptop to the oversized television we'd mounted on the wall last weekend, deciding that we couldn't deal with Sadie's 90s model constantly freaking out over too-quick cable speeds. We'd saved the older television for Tommy's room, when he got a little older. It even had one of those old VHS decks built into it. Perfect to show him all our old, terrible tv shows from days gone by.

Leo stepped in front of the television and lifted his chin, all pomp and circumstance. Tommy ran off to play while Sadie and I were seated upon the couch. I kicked my shoes off and she curled into the circle of my arm, tucking her head against my chest.

"Lady and gentlewolves," Leo began, bowing and sweeping his arm across his chest. "I present to you the fruits of my labor, the honorarium of my extraction, the-"

"Get on with it," Xav said, tossing an empty Coke bottle at his head.

It papled off his forehead and Leo scowled at him. "As I was saying. Our feature presentation."

He motioned at Gabe, who tapped a button on the keyboard. The television exploded with sad, barking dogs in filthy cages. There were cats in filth-caked hovels, all meowing at the top of their lungs. I frowned and pulled Sadie closer, but she was absolutely enthralled. There was anger on her face but an intensity in her gaze that I hadn't seen before. Fixing what she saw was what she lived for, was what everything she did was to work against.

And all she wanted to do was to climb through that screen and correct every issue she saw.

"The Fontaine Foundation is proud to present, Sadie's Sanctuary," said Leo's voice as the video swept away from the miserable animals.

Instead, we were treated to a video of the lodge. Land had been cleared, replaced with areas where dogs ran free and enormous bird aviaries. Cats enjoyed themselves as they clung to trees in fenced areas, exhibiting natural behaviors without the worry of becoming roadkill. Equines of various sorts, no unicorns of course, walked through endless pastures, all of them serviceable to feed the animals as they desired to eat.

From there, the video devolved into metrics and formulas, prices and buying structures that were in perfect synchronization with the land we had purchased. It maintained that we could work with a rescue of this size while maintaining our hunting land and our privacy.

Sadie's face lit up as she watched the presentation, her smile as wide as it could be by the end of it. It was something I hadn't considered. As much as I liked her little old house, she had certainly outgrown it and the property wasn't really big enough to expand the home any further.

If we wanted to continue to grow the pack or add adult members to it, we'd need more rooms. The lodge, with Lillian no longer a concern, was a perfect position to work from. And I thought the presentation was rather inspired, all things considered. Obviously, my pack had seen the potential that I hadn't.

It would work, if it was what Sadie wanted to do. We would never make her give up her cozy home. Maybe she could use it as an extension office, or a place to train people in her far-flung rescues, like the one coming along in Omaha.

"Can we really do that?" Sadie asked when the video held on our logo, my wolf's eyes staring at all of us.

Leo shrugged. "It'd cost a good bit to do it, but is it doable? Yeah, I called the county's building offices today and double-checked the zoning for the area. There's no one out there to complain, anyway, but you never know. Maybe the land next to us sells and they build right along the property boundaries."

Sadie blinked at him and smiled, then looked up at me for an explanation in plainer language.

Leo picked up on it before I could try to unwind what he'd said. "What I mean to say is, the zoning is fine. I'd just suggest staying a few acres off the property lines, just in case neighbors settle in next to us. Or, in the future, we may even buy that parcel, too." He paused, then gave her an anxious look. I could smell the worry roll off of him, like a boy who'd just picked a flower for a girl he had a crush on. All this time later and some of us were still in the honeymoon period.

"I think it's the most wonderful thing I've ever heard of and that you did an incredible job with that," Sadie said, pointing at the laptop. "I just don't understand all of it. There were a ton of figures in there and some of them didn't make sense to me. Could we review it tomorrow at work and get started on it? I think I've got more resources, calculators, and things like that, inside my desk."

He nodded, closing his laptop and destroying the link between it and the television. A football game popped up, some rerun from years ago. I dragged Sadie onto my lap and nipped the spot where I'd marked her. "Think we should distract him from work?"

The way the color worked its way from her neck and into her cheeks delighted me. I slid her shirt over her head and began work on her bra. "Gabe, I think Tommy could use a nap. Don't you?" I asked him.

Sadie shivered and wrapped her arms around my neck. "I think Tommy's had a very long, hard day."

"And hurry back down here," I told my cousin. "Before we forget to save you a spot."

Xavion and Leo joined us on the couch as Gabe grabbed our kid and ran upstairs. I made a careful mental note to invest in a decent screwdriver. We'd probably be breaking the frame on a lot of the furniture in the coming months and I didn't want to have to replace all of it just because the pack had enjoyed a party on them. Couches just weren't made like they used to be.

I lowered my head and kissed the top of the split between her breasts. Her sweet scent engulfed me and I closed my eyes, letting my fingers travel south, headed to a wonderful oblivion.

Chapter 20
Sadie

It took the better part of a year to finalize every plan we had for the lodge's transformation, but once we settled in, we moved like lightning.

Only in the last month of my pregnancy I'd had to stop helping, my alphas looking after me and the rest of the rescue while I lounged and scratched Carrie Ann's head. We recovered together, her surgery and my impending explosion of puppies, mostly through watching re-runs of Animal Planet feel-good pet shows.

I tucked my infant pups into their cribs, one right after another. Two girls, two boys, and none of us cared who had fathered who; though Xavion's son, Norrin, was darker than the rest and Leo's daughter, Analise, had his eye color. Jenelle and Caleb looked too much like both Gabe and Hudson, who favored each other anyway, to tell them apart. As a pack, we'd voted on names and it had been much easier that way.

I mean, until I delivered, we hadn't known that multiple alphas could father a litter. Most werewolves had one or two pups, that was it. But I'd been an oddity in my family, which was filled with a dozen aunts and uncles on either side throughout the generations. Maybe it just ran in my blood.

"Mommy, when they gonna be big enough t'hunt with the pack?" Tommy asked.

My brows raised down at him. "Is that the kind of thing we ask when people are in the house?"

He pouted, but I crouched down and whispered to him, "They'll be out with us by your next birthday. And maybe we'll all have a big romp in the woods, then. Would you like that?"

Tommy's birthday was only six months away, deep in the heart of fall. He beamed up at me and ran off, as young children tend to do, to tell his father. I watched him go, following him at a much slower step. I was still recovering from giving birth, a process that was so much more complicated when you were a shapeshifter, apparently. How many puppies had I delivered from rescue dogs and kittens from rescue cats? I knew the process deeply, intimately.

But it was different when it was you trying to catch your breath and bringing life into the world. I loved my kids, but I was pretty certain we were only doing that whole parade once, especially when we'd soon have four pups scampering around the house and Tommy to keep up with, too.

Then again, if someone had told me eighteen months ago that I'd be a werewolf, have pups of my own, and a pack of men who loved me, I would have laughed myself sick. You can never count on what the future holds, and it's so worth sticking around to experience it.

Norrin yawned, squirmed in his sleep, and I listened to the silence as my pups went quietly off to dreamland. Closing the door, and locking it, I headed out to see what my big, strong boys were up to.

Tommy, of course, had his father's ear. Hudson knelt, nodding as the boy chattered up a storm. He looked tired, but I expected that. "Any update on the site for the new factory?"

Hudson shook his head and picked Tommy up, the boy tucking himself against his chest. "No. The museum's team is supposed to be out there soon, but I guess some big storm stuck them in an airport. You're really sure we have to pay for paleontologists to dig up everything?"

"They aren't all paleontologists, my love. Some of them are aging experts and others are construction workers," I said, draping my arms around his neck. "It gets worse and worse as I go along. You want me to stop here?"

He shuddered. "All I hear is the museum saying 'cha-ching'. There's really no way to buy them off? We don't even know if that fossil is important."

"If they think it is, it is. You know how it works," I said, giving him a peck on the lips. "I know it's just a footprint, some kind of claw or something, but they say they've never seen it before."

"I wish them mud and endless rain," Gabe muttered, sitting on the wide deck at the back of the cabin.

I snorted. "Just takes longer to build the factory thattaways, you know it does."

My alpha shook his head. "It's a pain in the ass, is all."

"I do know a way to take your minds off it," I murmured.

Xavion, perched on the deck next to Gabe, looked up at me like I'd offered him a steak. Leo leaned against the railing, smiled, and closed his eyes. It was Hudson who nipped the nape of my neck, making me jump. "You tease us and you're going to get carried inside."

"Who says I'm teasing?" I grinned.

Tommy frowned between us, clearly disgusted with the lack of attention on him. "I wanna play video games."

Gabe, who had been prowling up on me from behind, peered over my shoulder and blinked. "Oh wow, buddy. I wanna play video games, too."

Kids. The perfect cockblock, but you can't hate them for it. Besides, his bedtime was in an hour and I knew that the longer my alphas had to wait, the more claw marks I'd leave in the headboard of our bed.

We spent the next hour entertaining the little guy, making sure he finished his supper, and watching the sun go down over the freshly budded trees and the frostless, muddy landscape. There were plans to start seeding pastures over the next month and I looked forward to the hours in the sun, watching my men strip naked to the waist, sweating and straining to grow grass for the livestock that had come along from the rescue.

I mean, what woman wouldn't want to see her man out there getting dirty, hot, grinding and plucking his way through the fields? Maybe they'd need to dump some water on themselves, get all wet and-

Whew. My mind was occupied with the most imaginative, incredible images I could possess as I put the dishes in the dishwasher. Hudson took Tommy up to bed and I spent a little time on the couch, alone, going over tomorrow's proposals for a new, sponsored veterinary practice and rescue combination that wanted to get ankle-deep in Fontaine's new philanthropy.

Over the past year, we'd sponsored over five hundred veterinary clinics, rescues, or local shelters around the world. We were still expanding, but it was a good start and I was proud of what I'd done. As it was, it also made sense to the finance guys that worked the floor down below me. They could take our charitable donations and apply it to taxes, something I'd never done when I ran my own rescue.

It meant huge savings that we could pass on to our customers and the farms that we worked with, always trying to grow and expand. We didn't want to take over the pet food industry, we just hoped that our policies would nudge it in a better direction; a direction that meant a happier life and lifestyle for everyone involved.

But the guys still tasted every new recipe and, to be honest, I did, too. Sometimes we brought a little home to Tommy to make sure that even picky dogs would eat it; because no one is pickier than a four-and-a-half-year-old. Of course, then we had to keep Tommy out of the food we kept around for the rescue dogs. It wasn't as if anyone saw him popping a kibble or two into his mouth and, to be honest, it wasn't out of place for little kids to do that now and then anyway.

We just preferred he didn't.

You know, just in case he decided to tell his new schoolmates later in the year.

Hudson snuggled down against the back of the couch, peeking at what I was reading. "Whatcha doin'?"

"Planning an extremely hostile takeover of the rescue industry, shutting them all down, buying them all out, and working to see if I can do the same to you," I said, smiling and looking back at him.

He grinned and shook his head. "Sounds sinister."

"Oh, it is. I'm a bad, bad girl."

His eyes narrowed and something dark touched his expression. "Do I need to put you in your place?"

I lifted my chin, kissing him and dropping the folder. He picked me up and carried me off to my pack, waiting in our bedroom as the last few rays of sunshine disappeared over the horizon.

I craved their attention and they were more than pleased to satisfy my urges. Since those first frantic few matings, we'd slowed down now and then from feral fucking to sweet, slow lovemaking; especially after they'd discovered that the pace drove me crazy and my begging got louder the slower they went.

My pack was the best thing that had happened to me, and they spent the next several hours reminding me of it.

True night found me out on the deck once again, a blanket around my shoulders as I watched the moon rise from the darkness. She was mostly full, yet not quite enough to turn me with Her gaze. Though I'd balked at the idea of moon worship early on, the rituals became clearer, felt more typical the longer I was with the pack.

Perhaps it was how some felt when they moved to another country or another culture within the same country. At first, everything was strange. The differences, while not bad, simply don't have the same meaning that they do to those around you. It isn't just that things are strange, but that *you* are a stranger.

Werewolf, human, neither likes to feel like they don't have a pack to belong to. You're a fish out of water, a lone wolf, worrying that you look like a fool to those around you. Or maybe, that you're making a fool of yourself and you'll never fix your reputation again.

Life is too short to worry about whether you're making the best impression all the time. We all make mistakes. Sometimes those mistakes do wonders for you. A puppy's mistake brought me and my rescue to the forefront of supernatural society and lifted us higher than I could have ever imagined.

But it isn't all about taking the world by storm or standing on a stage in front of everyone, telling them who you are and what it is that you do. It's about living, about finding your place on that stage and being content with it. You should always strive to be greater than what you are; it's practically melted into our DNA to work toward a better tomorrow. That doesn't mean that you do it at the cost of your own happiness.

So many do.

I lifted my head, closed my eyes, and scented the wind. A deer herd moved in the far forest, not yet leery of the werewolf pack that inhabited the woods at the moon's zenith. In the opposite direction, a raccoon wandered along trying to find early spring grubs. They would never become anything more than a raccoon's meal, too intent on being the worm the early bird got.

Well, raccoon.

Whatever.

Beyond my senses, I knew there were other werewolf packs. Beneath what made my pack *pack* was a core of something else. We were all made of the same person, once a man that had turned wolf and continued on with his life. He had made others, produced children, and those children had gone on to create more of us.

Lineage, at its core, was a soul-deep connection among the supernatural world. We all had it and I had only experienced it once in the past year, knowing my children before they were born in the same way I felt Hudson's exhaustion or Gabe's confusion when we were at work.

That bond was worth everything to me, the perfect connection that went so far beyond words that there were times when my pack and I simply listened to one another through it. And we didn't need to say that Tommy needed a bath or that one of us was stressed out. We just knew, and it was there, waiting for the pack to help.

It made the relationship that much easier, but it also made the relationship that much harder. There was no hiding from my pack, no sense of intimacy that they didn't know when we were close enough.

But I didn't want to hide anything from them. They knew me, really knew me.

And that was why I'd understood why Lillian had done what she did.

"If we could freeze to death, you'd have done it," Hudson muttered, sitting down beside me.

I leaned my head against his shoulder and continued to stare out into the night. "The deer are back again."

"We'll see what Tommy makes of them."

"Is he old enough?"

Hudson mmmed at me. "I was five when I took my first deer. The werewolf body grows much faster than the human one. We're predator-sized at four or five."

"They grow up so fast," I sighed.

"The alphas do. When we figure out what the pups' alignments are, I'm sure we'll be in for all sorts of interesting management. Omegas take a little longer."

"And betas?" I asked.

He paused. "I don't know any alpha-omega pair who have produced betas. They're very, very rare these days. But the betas I knew growing up more or less kept pace with the alphas. If we have a beta in there, they'll be loved. Life is harder for them, but they'll still be loved."

I nestled into his arms and there we sat, silent and watching the unmoving trees. We were lost forever in time, quiet and simply with one another. It had started like this, brought together by Tommy.

"Do you think we'll ever know if he really meant to do what he did?" Hudson cleared his throat. I turned and looked at him, frowning. "Hudson."

"I think it was likely he understood in a general way. He loved you from the moment he met you; and who wouldn't? But I don't know if he really got the complications with it. Everything turned out all right in the end, but he was a baby. He probably just saw what he wanted and went for it."

"Takes after his dad that way," I whispered, nudging him with my elbow.

Hudson tightened his grip on me and growled into my ear. "I don't mind proving it."

"I imagine that none of you mind proving it," I said. "But I think I'm worn out for the night. And there's work tomorrow. Eventually, even I have to sleep."

"Should I carry her majesty up to her rooms?"

I shook my head, smiling, and pulled my blanket away. I twisted just enough to wrap it around both of us. Though the chill in the air still didn't bother me, it was nice to have the trappings of a cool early spring night. At first, I'd gotten a few odd comments here and there when I'd been spotted without a jacket out in the snow. Apparently, people notice when it's 10 degrees out and you're still not cold.

But I still wanted to snuggle down in a blanket, have my hot cocoa, and wear fluffy jackets during the colder months. Maybe some part of me would always remain a little too human for conservative packs, but for my pack? I was the perfect fit.

In the end, I fell asleep against Hudson's chest and he carried me upstairs anyway. I only knew it because I woke up in the morning to an alarm clock that had been unplugged, the batteries removed from the device. I rolled out of bed, wandered through my usual routine of showering and feeding the pups before I fed Tommy and myself. The pack had decided I'd work from home until I'd fully recovered; and after that?

Lillian yawned as she walked past me, her hair a fluffy mess. "Hey, you need anything from the store today?"

She tickled Analise's chin before moving to grab a mug of coffee. I offered one out to her, already made the way she liked it. At once, she relaxed and took the cup from me.

"I don't think I do, but I'll check the list. Last I knew, we were pretty well set. There are three new dogs coming in today, though. I could use your help getting them settled in," I told her.

She sat down at the kitchen table and yawned again. "You got it."

It'd taken time, but it had turned out that Lillian had grown out of the convent life. She was still searching for what she wanted, but being surrounded with her own kind once again had helped her personality a great deal.

Trust was something that was earned, but she'd more than done her fair share. I left her alone with the kids, knowing deep down that she would never hurt them, and went out onto the deck once more, bringing my laptop with me. The world breathed rest, relaxation, and renewal. I had everything I needed; kids I loved, animals to care for, and a pack that adorèd me.

And I, them.

I inhaled, exhaled, and sat my cup down on the frostbitten deck. Then, I picked up my laptop and opened it up. My driving force in life had been, for as long as I remembered, to make the world a better place. I channeled it through my animal rescue, my passion, but there was still so much left to be done. There was still so much good that I could do for the world at large. I pushed the power button on the laptop and smiled.

It was time to get to work.

About the Author

Katelyn Beckett is the kind of woman who likes her coffee black, her stories dark, and her heroines strong. When not writing, she's usually busy adding to an endless pile of useless knowledge such as exactly how much force a couch can withstand and how to break out of cable ties. Katelyn writes Reverse Harem Romance with Happily Ever After endings guaranteed... eventually.

You can find Katelyn on Twitter @Kbeckettloves

Or on Facebook at Katelyn Beckett's Lovelies

Looking for another sweet temptation? Click here to head back to Katelyn's author page to find something else to make your toes curl ♥ . On Wings, Book 2 of Her Secret Menagerie featuring Eskal and his Nightflight is out now! Click here to grab your copy today!

Already missing the Fontaine pack? Puppy Problems, Sadie's Sanctuary Book #1, is out now!
https://www.amazon.com/dp/B08KJSG2GR

Printed in Great Britain
by Amazon

74324315R10119